Music in the Bone
and other stories

Marion Pitman was born rather randomly in Hertfordshire, but considers herself a Londoner, and lived in and around London until 2000, when someone burnt down her shop and flat. She now lives in exile in Reading. For many years she was talked out of being a writer, and has spent most of her life failing to make a living from the sale of second-hand and antiquarian books. She has also worked as an artists' model and edited a magazine for collectors. She has travelled to Zimbabwe, New Zealand and Sri Lanka to watch cricket, and would like to do so again. She has no car, no television, no cats and no money. Her grandfather was an engineer's pattern-maker, of which she is inordinately proud. Her hobbies include folk-dancing and theological argument, and she enjoys four degrees of separation from Schrödinger's cat. She also writes poetry, an activity she likens to the manufacture of high-class gas mantles.

Music in the Bone
and other stories

Marion Pitman

The Alchemy Press

Music in the Bone © Marion Pitman 2015

Cover design © Peter Coleborn

This publication © The Alchemy Press 2015

Published by arrangement with the author

All rights reserved. The moral rights of the author of this work have been asserted in accordance with the Copyright, Designs and Patents Act 1988

No part of the publication may be reproduced , stored in a retrieval system, or transmitted , in any form or by any means without permission of the publisher.

All characters are fictitious and any resemblance to real persons is coincidental.

FIRST EDITION

ISBN 978-1-911034-00-1

Published by The Alchemy Press
Cheadle, Staffordshire
www.alchemypress.co.uk

Contents

Cave Arborem	7
Music in the Bone	9
The Seal Songs	29
Amenities	39
Sunlight in Spelling	41
Disposal of the Body	59
Out of Season	65
Washing of the Water	81
Saxophony	85
Looking Glass	97
Christmas Present	101
Overnight Bus	105
Indecent Behaviour	121
Forward and Back, Changing Places	129
District to Upminster	143
The Cupboard of Winds	147
Contamination	159
Eyes of God	161
Dead Men's Company	167
Meeting at the Silver Dollar	185
Story Notes	195
Acknowledgements	199

Dedication

Absent friends (no ice)

"(Marion Pitman's) stories are about people who discover that the floorboards of reality are much thinner than they had supposed, and in some cases have been removed altogether."

— John Dallman.

Cave Arborem

That tree is twisted like a brown, arthritic hand
In any breeze, or none, it creaks and mutters to itself.
My Granddad, he once tried to cut it down —
The axe twisted from his hand, and nearly killed a dog.
My father tried to poison it —
The grass all round it died, the tree survived.

I pour wine about its roots,
Stroke its bark, and murmur soothing words;
Sit under it on sunny days, and sometimes moonlit
    nights,
Its trunk unsmooth and awkward to my back;
I listen when it mutters to itself,
In hopes one day of learning what it wants.

But when I know – ah, then what shall I know?

Music in the Bone

*Now your cage shall be made of the finest beaten gold
And the doors of the best ivory.*

The ballad finished, the woman sat down, and a man with a guitar stepped to the front of the room. Lena tried to stop fidgeting. Already she had pulled a thread in her skirt on a splinter from the table leg, and her restless fingers had encountered a mass of old chewing gum on the underside of the table top.

She took a tissue out of her bag, and spat, and wiped her fingers. She looked at her hands; they appeared grotesque and unnatural, like alien claws. She wondered if the stigmata were coming back. She caught a whiff of some foetid smell. Quickly she threw the tissue in the ashtray and put her hands in her pockets. Tom glanced at her, frowning. He was actually listening to this maundering sub-70s stream-of-consciousness lyric. One of the guitar strings was slightly flat, just enough to be painful.

The room was small, smoky and cold, with mismatched chairs, benches with holes in the red leatherette upholstery – revealing gross intestines of grey foam – and not enough people. Not surprising with this going on.

Her hands seemed to be wandering again, fiddling with the silver bird-skulls in her earlobes; she missed the intro to the next performer. She hadn't seen him before. He started to play the fiddle. His bow stroked and caressed the strings, producing sounds Lena had never heard from a violin. It purred, moaned, sighed; he made love to it, almost you heard the instrument reach orgasm.

When he finished, the audience was silent for a moment; then they applauded wildly. Lena was entranced. She had never heard an instrument sing so, heard music with such life and intensity.

His second number was a reel – quick, lively, vigorous. Images whirled in her head, wild dancing, lightning flashes, crashing surf and waterfalls; jungles of bright birds and vivid flowers.

When it ended she felt quite breathless, and joined in the applause with abandon.

He was cute, too. Tall, thin and wiry, black hair in long tangled curls, very white skin. Small silver rings glinted in his ears. He looked glamorous, in the magical sense: dangerous, feral. Probably, she thought, he would turn out to be a computer programmer for an insurance company, with no conversation beyond Windows and war-gaming. Still, he was a good deal more decorative than Tom. She glanced sideways at Tom's bald spot, the hair around it rough and in need of a trim. Not to mention a comb.

She generally went home with Tom after the folk club. That was as far as the relationship went, spending the night together once a week. It had been going on like that for months. She felt she couldn't bear it a moment longer. She would tell Tom she had a blinding headache, or the curse had come on early.

At one time she would have chatted up the fiddle player, tried to take him home with her, just for the hell of it. But that was in another life.

The club always finished by half-past ten so that the organisers could get back to some far-flung outpost of suburbia. Naturally most people drifted down to the still-open bar. Lena drifted with the rest. Tom was deep in discussion with a frowning woman in a long skirt; Lena caught the words "CD drive" and "mother board". She made an impatient move away from them and found herself next to the fiddle player.

He caught her eye and smiled.

She said, "I was very impressed by your playing. You're amazingly good," and thought, How naff does that sound?

But he looked pleased, and said, "Thank you."

She said tentatively, "I haven't seen you here before?"

"No. I only moved here recently."

"Oh, right." Pause. "Where were you before?"

"Oh, I've been living abroad."

"Uh huh?"

"Travelling."

"Right."

"Would you like a drink?"

"Oh! I'm sorry – I wasn't..."

"That's OK. But would you like a drink?"

"Thanks. I'll have a pint of Guinness."

He turned away to catch the eye of one of the young New Zealanders behind the bar.

Lena glanced round. The room was noisy, with the jukebox on, and a lot of girls in tight jeans and skimpy tops, drinking vodka or lurid cocktails, and having a good time judging by their loud voices. It seemed to be somebody's hen night.

She remembered a bar in – Dublin? Auckland? Cape Town? – sometime in another life. A live band playing very loud, dancing all night, spaced out on too much white wine and no food, heavily snogging an extravagantly under-dressed woman with red hair and big tits. She could remember the rum and coke taste of the redhead's mouth – nothing came of it. One of them had made a misstep, or they just hadn't wanted it enough. Where was she staying? A hostel, a five star hotel? It was all the same in those days. Another life. With the Latvian footballer in Sydney, looking for a bad time in King's Cross at four a.m. Christmas Eve in a sports bar in Wellington, high as a kite on fear and adrenalin. Another life.

The fiddle player turned with the Guinness. He smiled; his teeth were flat across the front, with long canines – not Dracula-long, just slightly wolfish. His eyes were a clear dark brown, like glasses of neat whiskey.

As she took the drink from him, she noticed his hands, pale and very thin, just skin strung over bones. She touched the back of his fingers; they were smooth, like alabaster, and nearly as cold.

"Thanks," she said with a smile, and looked into his eyes just a little too long.

They stood together in silence for a while; he drank beer; no-one spoke to them.

Then Tom called, "Lena! You coming?"

She turned. Now or never.

"Sorry," she said. "I've got a really early start tomorrow."

"OK. See you next week." And he was gone. Just like that.

Behind her, she heard a low, teasing voice: "Have you really got an early start?"

She turned back. He was looking at her with a smile twisting up one side of his mouth.

"Maybe," she said. "Maybe not."

"My name's Ed," he said.

"Lena."

"I only live round the corner. It's very near the tube

station."

"That's handy."

"Are you coming home with me?"

She stared at him. She no longer expected that sort of directness. He laughed. There seemed no reason not to say "Yes."

*

His flat was up three flights of stairs, an attic room with a sloping ceiling, and a low window that looked out on other roofs – all angles, different heights, red, brown, grey, black, tile, slate, concrete. Street lighting gave them an eerie glow.

The room was dimly lit, the walls hung with swags of black and dark-red cloth. A tall ebony and ormolu cabinet stood against one wall, on top of it a phrenology head, a malachite obelisk, a crystal ball on a blackwood stand, and one of those globes full of lightning that follows your hand. No stuffed crocodile, she thought; every alchemist's laboratory should have a stuffed crocodile.

Another wall was lined with instruments and sound equipment; against a third was a wide divan with a black silk spread.

Ed said, "What do you think?"

"Very Gothic," she replied. "You don't look Goth."

"Oh, you should see me at weekends." He laughed.

She looked along the wall. "You play a lot of instruments."

"Fiddle and guitar mainly. Keyboards now and then. I'm trying to learn the harp."

It was a small, portable, medieval-style harp, fancifully carved with wolves and unicorns.

"But the fiddle's my true love," he said. He put the case down on the bed and opened it, taking the cloth from the instrument and stroking its neck affectionately. It was a beautiful looking thing. The wood glowed with the patina of age and loving attention; the pegs, fingerboard and bridge were inlaid with ivory or bone, a warm yellowish white. The strings, and the hair of the bow, seemed to catch the light with a golden glint. She fancied it almost hummed softly to itself, there in the case.

"You're amazingly good," she said. "I've never heard anyone play the fiddle like that."

He grinned. "So you didn't say that just as a chat-up line?"

"Actually, no. I mean, yes. All right, it *was* a chat-up line, but it was true too."

He smiled again, slowly, suggestively, left the fiddle and moved towards her. He put his hands on her hips, lowered his head, and kissed her.

She gripped his elbows to steady herself; the kiss was long and deep, hungry, demanding. He tasted of beer and cigarettes. She found her whole body responding; her belly went on fire and yearned toward him At last he broke contact, and stepped back.

"D'you want a shower?" he said.

"Uh – no. I had one before I came out." She responded automatically then thought, That was wrong.

He said, "OK. I will, though." He kissed her lightly on the forehead, and went out through a curtained doorway in the corner.

Lena wandered around. She was shy of touching anything, but she looked avidly. On a battered map-chest beside the cabinet were a laptop and some papers; beside the instruments was a tall blackwood rack with several dozen CDs, many of artists she'd never heard of besides the likes of, Steeleye Span, Pink Floyd, Nick Drake, Counting Crows, Fields of the Nephilim. Eclectic, she thought. There was Bach, too, and Sibelius, and traditional

Irish fiddle players. There seemed to be several by a band called Procne.

When Ed came out she said, "Actually I think I might have a shower, if that's OK?"

"Sure," he replied. "Plenty of hot water."

She showered quickly, trying to keep her hair dry, leaving her earrings in. Her heart beat too fast, her stomach fluttered, nervous as a schoolgirl on a first date. She laughed at herself.

She came back to the bed-sitting room wrapped in a towel. Ed was naked, sitting back on the divan. He pressed a remote control and music filled the room.

It was a fiddle, backed by keyboard and a flute or whistle. It sounded like Ed's playing.

She sat on the edge of the bed and said, "Is that you?"

"That's Procne," he replied, "which is me."

"Just you?"

"Just me."

"Is that a flute?"

He got up and stepped across to the instrument wall, and opened a small case. He took something out, returned, and handed her a short cylinder, smooth and dull white. It was pierced like a tin whistle, but the shape was rough and irregular.

"It's a thigh bone," he said.

"A human one?"

"Of course not." He was smiling; she wasn't sure whether to believe him.

"It's a native artefact," he said. "It makes an incredible sound." He put it to his mouth and blew softly. The notes that came out were beautiful, pure, eerie, chilling. Lena felt the hairs on her arms bristle; there was darkness in the sound, and the warning of a deadly snake unseen among leaves...

He stopped playing and saw her expression.

"Don't you think it's wonderful?" he asked.

"Yes. But scary."

He looked at her, his head on one side, then he put the flute away, backtracked on the CD, and unwound her towel. His response to her nakedness was immediate, and her own body also responded at once; she wanted him instantly, urgently. The music intensified the mood; it throbbed and wailed with aching sexual need, with pounding blood.

He laid her on the divan. His caresses became rough; he bit her breasts and she cried out at the pain, but was too deep in the grip of lust to push him away. His hands were hard, but she thrust against them, relishing the force of resistance.

Under and behind all, the music beat with the rhythm of sex, with deep lascivious notes that seemed to curl up like tongues of fire, igniting sparks all through her limbs.

But still, at the last moment, with a reflex she stiffened and pulled back, and said, "Condom."

"What?" He sounded genuinely bemused.

"Condom. I'm not on the pill. There's some in my bag if you..."

He gave a small, rather bitter laugh, and reached out to a cabinet beside the bed. He looked at her while he put on the condom by touch. There was something in the dark eyes she couldn't quite fathom; was it just naked desire, or was there something else...?

But she forgot it all once he began thrusting with the underlying beat of the music, which had moved on to a faster, simpler, more rhythmic track – almost, had she been able to think about it, as if he had compiled the tracks to the pace of his lovemaking.

*

Afterwards she felt not so much satisfied as drained, sucked dry. For several minutes she couldn't move.

He said, "Do you want to stay the night?"

"Uh..." She didn't really; she felt insecure, these days, sleeping away from her own place, but— "What time is it?"

"Two thirty."

"D'you mind if I stay?" She really didn't think she had the strength of mind - or body - to go anywhere right now.

"Sure. That's OK. I'll have to throw you out early, though - I have to go to work."

"OK."

He showered again, but Lena scarcely had the energy to stagger to the toilet. Unlike most men, Ed seemed energised by sex; he was playing something low and sinister on the flute when she fell asleep.

He woke her early, as he had said; he seemed anxious to see her go, so she showered quickly, drank the coffee he brought, left without mentioning breakfast.

As she started down the stairs she passed a woman in a light raincoat - slim and pretty, with heavy blonde hair falling to her shoulders - who stared hard and hostilely at Lena as they passed, and Lena thought she heard a short, ironic laugh behind her.

*

When she got home, Lena went to change her clothes. She was startled and rather appalled at the number of small bruises on her arms and breasts, stomach and thighs. She didn't remember acquiring all those. She felt stiff, too, as if she had fallen, or slept on a hard floor.

She ran a bath - she still had over an hour before she needed to leave for the café; she wasn't on breakfasts this week. She wondered about Ed. On the whole, she thought she'd rather not see him again. The sex had been amazing; he was interesting company – and a brilliant musician, and she was always taken by people who were very good at what they did – but she didn't like feeling that far out of control. Still, the question was unlikely to arise; in Lena's experience, men who took you to bed the first time you met seldom wanted to repeat the event. So although he'd taken her phone number, she wasn't surprised not to hear from him. She missed the folk club the next week, and when she went the week after it was only with the faintest expectation of seeing him.

Tom had phoned three times. She had tried to put him off, but in the end she said she wanted a break from the relationship. Since Tom had never admitted that they had a relationship, he tried to argue with this. He said, "I suppose you've dropped me for that poncey fiddle player."

She said, "Don't be silly," and put the phone down.

Should she make up with Tom? She was certainly in charge of the relationship, such as it was, but he bored her so. She thought of Ed playing the thigh-bone flute and was shocked at the flood of lust that provoked. Well, she said to herself, that would wear off.

*

Ed wasn't at the club when she arrived, and she wasn't sure if she were disappointed or relieved. But when he turned up in the interval, with the blonde from the staircase, she was definitely angry. He sketched a wave and a smile. She raised an eyebrow, said, "Hi," brusquely, and went down to the bar.

She sat there for three-quarters of an hour, drinking gin, and fantasising that he would come down alone and speak to her and explain and apologise; then she went home. The pain was astonishing.

Dammit, she thought, I don't even like him. But he could have rung and warned me. Except a man wouldn't see the necessity. Not after a one night stand. Meaning nothing. And it meant nothing to me either – God knows I'm old enough to know how these things work.

She started to shake, and went to lie down. Her hands itched and smarted dreadfully.

All night she dozed and woke to the sinuous sounds of the flute and the fiddle, sounds that seemed to have wound themselves around her brain cells. With some idea of laying the ghost, she went out on her break next day and looked in a record shop for Procne. There was nothing. She asked the assistant, but there wasn't anything in the catalogue. Didn't mean a thing of course; he probably just sold the CDs at gigs.

The next week she wondered whether to give the folk club a miss. Tom wasn't talking to her, and she didn't know if she could handle the humiliation of Ed's turning up with the blonde again.

In the end she went late, arriving after the interval. She slipped in during the applause. Ed was playing. He had the guitar this time. His fingers flew over the strings, as his left hand hunched and squeaked on the frets; the notes seemed sharp and glittering like shards of glass, weaving a circle, a crown of thorns, a stifling circumference of ice, dazzling in the sun. It hurt.

When he finished, the applause was deafening. He glanced up – Lena couldn't tell if he saw her or not. She looked around, but couldn't see the blonde.

He put down the guitar and picked up the fiddle, tuned it, and began a slow air, yearning, languorous, full of hope and despair and uncertainty. Despite herself Lena found tears in her eyes.

The audience was silent for several beats after he

finished, and the applause was quieter, but went on and on.

He stepped off the stage and came across to where she was standing. "Hi," he said. "Sorry about last week."

"You could've warned me," she said, resisting the impulse to say, Oh, that's all right.

He frowned; "I suppose so."

"So is that your girlfriend? I saw her before, at your flat."

He shrugged. "She's just a friend. So are you – I hope."

She looked into his eyes and felt her stomach churning. Her mind was saying, He can't just dismiss it like that, but her body wanted him, on almost any terms.

He said, "Will you come back with me tonight?"

She found herself saying, "Yes."

*

They left early, and when they arrived in the flat he poured glasses of whiskey; they sat on the divan sipping the drinks. He took the guitar out of the case, and began changing a string. The new string, out of a cloth bag with no label, glinted in the soft light of the lamps. The frets of the guitar were inlaid with strange angular patterns. He saw her looking at them, and pointed. "Mystic runes," he said, "in an unknown language." She raised an eyebrow, and he laughed. "It's supposed to be Arabic or something. Probably says Made in Japan."

Something rang false in his tone. She said, "All your instruments are unusual some way."

He gave a one-sided smile. "I guess I'm trying to find the perfect instrument. The guitar's good; the fiddle's better. The flute's got its own – uh – something, but it's a bit primitive. Maybe I'll find what I'm looking for with the harp."

"And what are you looking for?"

"Ah!" He gave her a big, genuine smile. "That's the sixty-four thousand dollar question. I can only say I'll know it when I find it... I don't know – the essence of music? The thing that all music reminds us of – the soul of music? The music of souls, perhaps?

"As you say, I ... well ... modify my instruments, trying to get closer to – to the heart of music, the real thing. That's more than just sound, that's being, meaning, essence ... then you'd hear something."

"But how do you do it? How do you 'modify' them?"

"Ah that, I'm afraid, is a trade secret. One day I'll tell you, I think. Maybe you'd understand – better than Heather."

He looked at her, and she thought, Is that meant to make me feel better about Heather? But it did, all the same. He put on another Procne CD, a gentler one this time, with a good deal of keyboard, which seemed to calm and dilute the effect of the fiddle and guitar. The flute was scarcely in evidence.

Lena took the first shower; he lent her a red silk dressing gown. While he was in the bathroom she wandered around. Feeling daring, she tried the top drawer of the map chest, but it was locked. She picked up a cassette tape that lay on top behind the printer; the hand-written label said, "Edward Oliver – First Album". As she turned it to read the list of tracks, his voice, sharper than usual, said, "Put that down!"

She dropped it and stepped back, reddening. "I'm sorry – "

"No. Sorry. I – that's a very early tape, and very bad. I'm rather sensitive about it."

He put his hands on her shoulders, and looked into her eyes, and she forgot the tape. The sex, like the music, was slower and gentler this time, though Lena still found herself with bruises she couldn't account for. Afterwards she drifted imperceptibly into sleep.

*

They saw each other after that once or twice a week. She didn't know if he was still seeing Heather, and didn't ask. Sometimes the sex was gentle and easy; more often it was increasingly violent. Sometimes he would put his hands on her head and press down and back till she was worried her spine would snap. He was strong, and she was afraid to struggle too much. He pinched and bit her breasts, although she asked him not to. But then he would tease her until she went into orbit, making her wait for the climax, and at last igniting a pit of fire deep inside her that no-one before had ever reached; and the pain would seem unimportant.

Sometimes he would play the fiddle or the guitar before they began. If he played the flute, things were more likely to get out of hand. She never heard him play the harp.

"I'm still working on it," he said.

Every time she got home, stiff and sore and black and blue, she thought, Why the hell am I seeing him; but when he rang she still said Yes, and when he played she felt helpless to resist anything he wanted.

The palms of her hands stung continually; the stabbing pain in her side was back.

They didn't go out together. Once she suggested – just casually – going to a movie. His eyes veiled, and he shrugged. "Sorry," he said, "I don't get much free time."

"Oh." She was startled, but he quickly went on to talk about something else.

So she went home with him after the folk club, just as she had with Tom. At other times he rang quite late in the evening, when it was too late to go out anywhere, and she went to his flat. She never said, "Why don't you come over here?" She knew he wouldn't.

Sometimes they had a take-away meal, often a bottle of wine. But most often he played music and did extraordinary, painful, amazing things to her body.

Once she stood at the window of the flat in a summer twilight, looking out at the planes and angles of the roofscape, and said, trying to sound playful, "So what do you do in real life?"

"I work in IT," he said, "and it's very, very, boring, and I don't talk about it in my own time."

So she couldn't ask him any more.

*

One night he played a throbbing, dark track, with an insistent beat and the flute underlying everything. The fiddle was strident, the guitar plangent; the whole pulsed with menace. Ed was holding her head and nibbling her neck and shoulders, his hands stroking her sides, relaxing her, when suddenly she felt a pain so sharp her body jerked upright reflexively as she screamed, wrenching his hand away, her head hitting the bridge of his nose.

He yelled, "What the fuck?" as he reared back, both hands to his face, blood pouring between them.

She sat, gasping, one hand to her shoulder where his teeth had met and blood trickled down. He threw his head back, and managed at last to stem the nose-bleed. Half stunned still, she helped him clean up. Then they stood in the bathroom and looked at each other.

"What the *hell* did you do that for?" he said.

"I couldn't help it. That *hurt*."

"Are you telling me you don't like pain? You stupid bitch, you're longing for it – I can smell it, I can taste it, it comes off you in *waves*. You deafen the air with your need for pain."

"But not from *you*, not from *you*." Feet, hands and side throbbed as she spoke.

He shook his head. "Such a pity. I know I could have made it work with you. You're so strong. You don't know what you missed. I'll have to do the best I can with Heather."

She heard the words but didn't take them in.

Suddenly, he leaned forwards, picked off with his nail the dried blood over the wound on her shoulder, blood welling up. Before she could react, he pressed a tissue to the wound, and took it back, red and wet, saying "A souvenir."

All she could think of was getting away from him. She backed into the bedroom, but he made no attempt to follow. Pain hammered so hard in her palms she could scarcely get dressed. She finally managed it, picked up her coat and bag, and hobbled out. He leaned in the bathroom doorway; but as she started down the stairs she heard him playing the flute. She forced her hands over her ears.

*

Time went by. Ed didn't call. Lena left the answering machine switched on, terrified of what would happen if she heard his voice. She avoided the folk club. Tom started phoning again, saying he was worried about her. She told him she had a new job, working evenings.

Her boss at the café said, "I don't know what you've been on, love, but you did right to give it up."

Gradually the throbbing in her hands subsided. She thought about what Ed had said, and tried to avoid thinking about pain.

*

After about three months, a friend just returned from Australia rang and asked Lena to come to the folk club. Lena tried to put her off, but Jenny was very forceful; Lena wasn't feeling forceful. In the end she said, "Look, Jen, there's a chap goes there sometimes that I don't want to see. I haven't been for months."

"What, just because of some bloke? Why? What did he do?"

He bit me. No, she couldn't say that. "Well – um – we were seeing each other, and it ended badly."

"Tom?"

"No, not Tom. Another bloke."

"Well, for God's sake, Lena, you can't run your life by blokes you're avoiding. Anyway, he might be avoiding you – you won't know if you never go."

In the end she agreed to go. At least Jenny would be some protection.

They got there early – another of Jenny's irritating habits. Ed was sitting on the edge of the stage, talking to Rob. Rob knew Jenny; before Lena could protest she was dragged across the room.

Beside Ed on the stage stood the harp.

Ed said, "Hallo, Lena."

To her great relief, she didn't go into rabbit-with-snake mode. Had she overestimated the power of his voice?

She said, "Hallo. Have you finally got it together with the harp?"

He smiled. "I hope so." He stood up, and moved between her and the instrument. "It would have been better with you."

"What? What would?"

"If you'd stayed. It would have been better. But I think I've got it right."

He moved just a little, so she could see the harp.

She said, "You've finished customising it, then?"

"Modifying. I prefer modifying."

The wood glowed, what little one could see for the

intricate, off-white inlay, bone or ivorine, the pattern something like Celtic knotwork, endlessly interwoven, polished and shining. The pegs were of the same material. The strings glowed softly, with an organic more than a metallic gold. The only thing that marred its perfection was a small dark smear, the colour of dried blood, on the sound-bow.

Lena found it hard to take her eyes off it. It seemed to be mesmerising her as much as Ed had. Someone spoke to Ed; people moved, interrupting her view of the harp, and she managed to tear herself away, and went for a drink. She returned after the session had started, and stood at the back. Jenny was deep in conversation, talking to a woman with a high, thin and barely audible voice.

Lena was aware of impatience, a feeling of marking time, until Ed played the harp. After a bit she found a seat near the front, on the other side of the room from where Ed was. He performed last before the interval, sitting down and setting up the harp on a stool. As he drew his fingers across the strings, everyone in the room fell silent, even the couple who stood at the back and had talked through every song since 1972. Lena lost all sense of time and space. She felt blinding sunlight, another time and place, and the impossible high of that week with Peter, and the intolerable pain that followed; felt as she had not allowed herself to feel since; felt again the intense joy of seeing his face, of his voice, that made her spine tingle; the smell of his skin, the smooth black skin of his shoulder, in a green singlet; he was there, he was turning towards her, smiling —

— and the music stopped, and her eyes darkened, and her body fell through fathoms —

— and she opened her eyes, and Ed was setting the harp upright on the stool, and the audience was still silent, too stunned for applause.

And then the harp sang. It sang with a woman's voice, and Ed wasn't touching it, he sat frozen, a look of utter dismay on his face. The harp sang:

He stole my bones for ivory
He stole my hair for gold
He stole my blood for fire and flood
He tried to pour away my soul
He scoured my bones, he wove my hair,
He poured my living blood through air
He burned my flesh, he poured my life away
To weave a net, a net to trap
The music of the universe
The sound of heaven, the sound of earth
The music of the soul —

It ended with a single piercing note, like a cry of intense pain—

—and she knew. She knew what had happened to the woman on the stairs, and why she wasn't here. She knew what the harp was inlaid with - felt it, excruciatingly, in her bones. She knew what it was strung with - but surely the gold hair had been too short...

Ed was staring, his face white as bone, his eyes burning.

"I wanted it to be you," he said. "It would have been so much better with you. It should have been you..."

Lena looked away, before she read what was in his eyes. She stood, and walked out of the still silent room. In the corridor she paused. The pain in her hands was gone.

Jenny came out after her. "My God," she said, "what was that about? Lena - you all right?"

She took a deep breath." I'm fine. Jen, I want you to come with me to a police station."

The Seal Songs

Ewan could hear his father calling him in but he was listening to the singing, and his father always left him alone when he was listening to the singing. At first he had used to hit him, but now he left him alone. Ewan sometimes wondered why.

The singing came out of a low, green hill; the voices were very high and clear and sweet, unlike his father's voice, which was loud and unmusical, and harsh with anger and tiredness. Presently the calling stopped, and Ewan guessed from experience that his father had seen him and gone away, and that soon he would go into the village to get drunk.

*

When Calum MacNeill had finished the mainland education his father had worked so hard to give him, he had returned to the island intending only to say goodbye to his father and visit his mother's grave, before taking his law degree to London. But his father was ill, and Calum had stayed. After his father had died, and the lonely green island and the great green and blue and white Atlantic, and the lovely Fiona MacIain, had all put their spell on Calum, he had stayed to marry her and to work his father's croft. But Fiona's beauty had been of the delicate kind, and she had not lived to see her fair boy baby grow. So here was Calum MacNeill at thirty-two, breaking his back to make a bare living, with no law practice, and no wife, a patch of black earth and a handful of livestock, and a son he was afraid of.

For Ewan had inherited his mother's ear, the Gift of

Ewan MacIain, his ancestor and namesake, and Ewan listened to things his father could not hear, and his father was afraid.

*

When the singing stopped, Ewan went home and put himself to bed. He slept too soundly to wake when his father came in. In the morning his father said, "You didn't come in last night when I called."

"No, Father."

"You were listening to that damned devil-music you pretend to hear, weren't you, boy?"

Ewan went on with his work, made no reply. His father shouted louder. "You're as bad as the old woman – mad, like her!"

"Which old woman is that, Father?"

"You know damn fine! Old mad Ishbel MacLean, your mother's cousin that sings to the seals. You're mad, your mother was mad – God rest her – all of us on these islands are mad! Them that go have the right of it – I should never have come back!" And he flung out like a storm gale.

Ewan finished the housework quickly, went out, saw his father with his back turned to him, and slipped silently away, making for the other side of the island, for the croft of Ishbel MacLean. He had not known the old woman sang to seals – he was intrigued. Twice, when his father was not about, Ewan had heard the seals sing. He had tried to remember their songs, which were deeper, more melodious, and more human in their feeling and their words than the heart-aching, otherworldly songs that came from the green mounds and knolls; but he could only recall snatches and fragments. Ewan liked to sing, but when he sang his father hit him – so he sang the songs he heard from the hills only when he was alone. He learnt other songs, in English, during term-time in the tiny island school, but he never sang them on his own, and his father never heard them. The songs in the hills, and those the seals sang, were in the language Ewan had learnt from his grandmother, who had looked after him when he was small, and from a few old people on the island; but the schoolteacher and Ewan's father both made him speak English.

But now was the long summer holiday when Ewan, at every chance, sought out the emptiest parts of the empty island and walked and sang and dreamed.

On the wide white western shore the sand squeaked underfoot like birds chirping. When there was a steady wind, which was almost always, the grains of sand sang as they tumbled over each other. Sometimes Ewan fancied the singing of the sand was the loneliest sound in the world, but he preferred the loneliness of the endless beach, and the endless sky, and the sea that rolled unbroken to America, to the loneliness of the dark house with his father's eyes on him, and even that to the hideous isolation of the school, where the teacher waited to pounce and call him wicked and stupid and impertinent, and to make mirthless fun of him, and the other children waited to laugh and jeer and taunt him. Ewan felt he would not have minded so much if he could have discovered a reason for these things; but he could not.

They kept a mouse in a cage in the classroom, and one day, Ewan's mind wandering a moment from the lesson, he had seen the cage open and the mouse gone. He had said, "Please, miss—"

But before he had got any further: "Ewan MacNeill, you will not interrupt when I am speaking. I realise that your own knowledge is so extensive that you have nothing to learn from anything I may say, but you must remember that not everyone has the benefit..." and so on, until a girl screamed and giggled as she saw the mouse running across the floor. A red-headed boy called Angus had caught the mouse and locked it up again. And the teacher had told everyone to calm down, and thanked Angus and said how clever and helpful he was, and looked at Ewan as if he had let the mouse out in the first place.

It did not make sense to Ewan. But here on the glittering sand, where the islanders had once dug for cockles, it didn't seem to matter very much.

He was not alone: the island wore a circlet of gulls about its head, screaming against the wind, and out at sea the whiskered heads of seals bobbed like so many old men bathing. Once, Ewan had stood so still so long that one of the seals had come out of the sea and waddled up the beach, to touch his leg with its nose. Ewan had stroked its shiny wet head, and knelt down, and they had looked each other in the eyes for half a minute before the seal turned and bounced back down and into the water. After that Ewan had not felt so lonely. Once he dreamt that his mother was a seal.

*

Ewan sang now, tramping across the island, the familiar wind whipping the hair into his eyes. He crossed the glen where men and women were cutting and drying and carting away the jet-black peats – most of them tossed him a greeting and Ewan would murmur something, and when he had passed they turned to each other and shook their heads. But Ewan walked on, and scrambled nimbly, with the easy assurance of long custom, up the steep, rocky side of the hill, and wandered unhurried down the long, gentler slope of the other side, where the little black milch cows grazed. And the wind smacked of the sea as he came to the ruffled blue loch, beside which huddled the low stone cottage of Ishbel MacLean.

Ishbel MacLean was very, very old; her face was pale, her skin like crumpled paper that had been smoothed out, seeming too big for her bones. Her eyes were very distant, as if her soul were barely in her body any longer. She was long widowed, her children all dead or gone away, and all but one of her grandchildren gone to sea, or to the mainland for work, or flown like wild geese to America. The old woman hardly moved, now, from the seat where Ewan found her, blinking his sunlit eyes against the sudden inside darkness.

The old woman did not move, but she heard him enter, and called out in a thin voice like wind in long grass, "Who is there?"

"Ewan, son of Calum MacNeill," said Ewan. "I would be learning something from you, Mrs MacLean."

"Come in, and welcome, Ewan mac Calum MacNeill," she said. "I am old, and I don't see you well, and I cannot stand; but you go over to the table, there is milk and cake for a guest."

Ewan thanked her, and accepted the refreshment, and said, "My father says that you sing to the seals. I have heard the seals sing, but I can't remember what I hear. I shall be glad if you will teach me some of their songs."

Her eyes brightened; she smiled a little. "So, you hear them – and some say the seals do not sing, and it is all fancy. Sit, child, sit down."

Ewan picked up a low stool, and set it on the sanded floor at the old woman's feet. "I hear a lot of singing," he said. "It's very beautiful, but my father doesn't like it."

"Whom do you hear singing?" she asked, in a strange tone.

Ewan finished the cake and licked his fingers. "I hear people singing in the knolls. I don't know who they are, because if I ask my father he hits me; and if I mention it at school, the teacher's angry, and the other children laugh. And anyway my granny always said I shouldn't ask.

"I think I should like to be a seal," he went on, thoughtfully. "They're beautiful, and they're gentle-looking, and so silky smooth, and graceful in the water. It must be wonderful to be moving so easily through the water – a bit like flying – and never to be beaten, and never to have to go to school. And I like fish."

The old woman was thoughtful too. She said, "Ewan, I haven't much to do in the world now, and I remember best things that happened long ago, but is not your mother a MacIain?"

"She was Fiona MacIain. She died when I was a baby. Why?"

Ishbel MacLean smiled and nodded. "Then you too have the gift. For I was a MacIain, before I married. And your name is Ewan! Then certainly I must teach you the seal songs."

"But first, please," said Ewan, "who is it that sings in the hills? And what is the gift? And why doesn't my father like it? I've heard him saying, 'Damn old MacIain and his gift', but he doesn't say what he means by it."

So Ishbel MacLean told him, how the fair folk, the sith, live in the green mounds and the hollow hills; and often their singing can be heard by those with the ears to listen. And she told how Ewan's distant ancestor, Ewan MacIain, had come one day upon a woman from the mound, that is, a woman of faerie, and had listened to her singing till she saw him. And when she saw him she was angry that he had watched her unseen. But MacIain praised her singing with many fine words and what was more important, meaning every one of them (for she was not one to be impressed by long words), and he pleased her, and instead of cursing him she gave him three gifts: that he and all his children would always have the friendship and good will of the fair folk, and always be able to hear their singing, and have the singing voice.

"And some say also that Ewan MacIain's wife was a seal woman, but I don't know the rights of that."

Ewan said, "I don't understand."

The old woman sighed. "There's no-one knows the old tales now, or holds the old beliefs. Well, some will say that the seal folk can come ashore at will, and shed their seal skins, and take the shape of human men and women, but if they return to the sea they must be seals again forever. On another island, they say that they are the sons of a king, under an enchantment, and can only return to their human forms at night. And my grandfather said they were the souls of those lost at sea, and that is why you must be good to them, because they might be your friends and kinsfolk.

"But my mother was used to say – and she was a MacCodrum, and they are related to the seals, you know – *she* said that the seal people are first cousins to the people of the mounds. As to your father – I expect he can't hear the singing, and that's putting the fear on him, for many people are afraid of what they don't know."

"That sounds rather silly," said Ewan, "but it's hard on him not to hear it. And now, teach me the seal songs, please."

So she taught him the seal songs, full of the deep sea and the ocean swell, and beauty that was less and more than human; and many other songs she had learnt from the fair folk. And Ewan sang the songs he had heard, and by the time Ewan left the old woman, still singing, to go home, it was coming on dark.

*

Calum had walked out his rage, and thought miserably, "*Is* he mad? Should he be put away – or see a psychiatrist – out here? Ridiculous." He remembered an old man who'd lived on the island when he, Calum, was a boy: Crazy Iain, Poor Old Crazy Iain to some of the women. He was pitied and tolerated, and he had terrified Calum. Calum's childhood seemed to have been compounded of fears – fear of his father's austere anger, and now and then a beating, carried out with a horrible calm; fear of his mother's tears; fear of Poor Crazy Iain, his awkward gait, and distorted, hollow voice; and fear of the countless, faceless powers that thronged the earth and air and sea. But in his expensive school and university, Calum had come to feel secretly superior to his parents, and so for the first time to love them a little; to regard Crazy Iain as an unfortunate product of in-breeding; and to dismiss the faeries and phantoms as fancy and superstition. So it never occurred to him now to think that Ewan's singers might exist; but he was afraid of them just the same.

Calum reminded himself there was work to be done, and slowly turned back. The flowered island laid out all around him the beauty that had seduced his youth, but Calum was disillusioned with beauty. Damned wind, he thought, wind and rain and damned hard work – why the hell do I stay?

He could not remember the day Fiona died, but he had got seriously drunk for the first time in his life, and stayed drunk for a week. When he was finally sober he was drained of all will and desire, of everything but pain; when they said he must see to his land and care for his son, he obeyed, and Fiona's mother looked after the baby while Calum drowned his grief in work till the day was gone, and then drowned it in whisky. And one day he woke up and found the pain was gone, and so was half he knew of law, and he couldn't care for the books that lay dusty on shelves; and he found a son he knew nothing about, who listened to inaudible voices. He thought of leaving the boy and fleeing back to the mainland, but Fiona seemed to sing in the wind and smile in Ewan's face, and Calum couldn't leave.

But now the memory of Fiona's face was masked by that of Crazy Iain, and as Calum tried not to hate his son, a voice whispered, "You killed her. You killed her," and another replied, "No – the boy. He killed her. He killed her – the boy."

*

When Ewan reached home it was late, and his father was home, and drunk, and he cursed Ewan, and beat him for staying away all day; but Ewan did not really pay him very much attention, for his head was full of songs.

The next day was Sunday, and on Sundays Calum MacNeill never got drunk until he and Ewan, washed and brushed and in their good clothes, had been to Mass. After a bad Saturday night Calum was apt to fancy that the prayers sounded blasphemous on Ewan's lips, or even that the words in the boy's mouth were turning subtly into faerie songs, to entice all the souls of the congregation down into hell.

This Sunday, after the service, Calum stopped to talk to one or two neighbours; when he turned back to Ewan the boy was not there. Someone said she had seen Ewan wander down towards the beach, so Calum MacNeill also walked that way.

He came down the dunes to the long stretch of white shore, where the gulls cried lonely overhead, and he saw his son Ewan lying flat on his face, in his good clothes, on the wet white sand; and in a clear high voice Ewan was singing, in the Gaelic, a song that set up shivers down

Calum MacNeill's spine and all over his body. Calum had always insisted that the boy speak English, but in any case he could not listen to the words for that haunting, beautiful, terrible tune. He prayed God to make it stop.

A little way out in the glittering water ran a line of skerries – rocks that stand out from the sea but are covered at high tide. The tide was low now, and on the skerries three great, grey seals were sunning themselves. Calum was not afraid of the seals, for he thought of them only as animals. He had never heard them sing.

Calum looked at the seals, smooth and shining and sleek, with their great soft eyes and sad, intelligent faces turned landward, and gradually it dawned on him that Ewan was singing to them, and that they were listening. And just as he realised that, Ewan stopped singing, in the middle of a phrase, and the nearest seal rose on its front flippers, lifted its nose, and to Calum's intense horror, took up the song where Ewan had left off.

It was too much. For a moment Calum MacNeill became purely mad with fear. He gave a terrible scream, at which the three seals split the water and vanished. He picked up Ewan by his collar and waistband, lifted him, swung him, and hurled him out to sea. And then truly the madness came on Calum MacNeill.

For what he seized and flung from him was a small boy; and what flew through the air silently, without a single cry, and curved down towards the Atlantic's blue surface, was a small boy. But what struck the water and slipped noiselessly under the wave was a small, grey seal.

Amenities

"There's pieces of string on that picture rail", said Mrs Debenture, "that've been there since 1862."

"Really? What happened in 1862?"

"They invented Christmas decorations."

"Did they? Does no-one ever take down last year's string?"

"Why? It's not unhygienic, string."

"I suppose not. Just a bit – cluttered."

"Plenty of room up there for more string."

"I suppose there is."

"And this is the scullery. Those mousetraps go with the house. You'll need them. Did you know that if the offspring of one pair of house mice during an average lifespan were laid end to end, they'd reach from here to the sun? Mind you, I don't know who's tried it."

When we got to the main bathroom she started on soap.

"The old squire didn't hold with soap. He said he never used soap on his horses, and a good rub down and a curry comb were good enough for him. The mistress pointed out that we did wash the horse blankets, so he agreed to change his clothes once a month. They occupied separate rooms."

"I suppose separate bedrooms weren't uncommon in those days."

"They also occupied separate bathrooms, separate dining rooms and separate sitting rooms. They used to say you could smell the old squire a mile off."

"When was all this?"

"1957. Of course the squire didn't die until 1973. I came here in '57. Miss Debenture I was then – I never married, but cooks and housekeepers are always 'missus'. It's to do with the authority, you see. Missus gives you the social gravitas."

"So when they make you housekeeper, do they give you a wedding ring, or do you have to buy your own?"

"Look, dear, that's just the way it works. Now *this* is the powder closet where the squire's grandfather did away with the parlour maid. 1789, that was."

"The squire's *grandfather*?"

"Very long lived family. He was quite a young man at the time. Of course he wasn't hanged for it – the coroner was a member of the hunt, so they brought it in accidental death. And that's where they buried the ape, after it ravished the squire's mother and she broke its neck."

"I see."

"The law was more sensible in those days. Now there's rules and regulations; you can't bury dead bodies less than so many feet from the house, and so on and so forth. In the old squire's day a man's land was his land and a man's dead body was his dead body."

"I believe in law you cannot make testamentary disposition of your own body because you have never owned it as a dead body."

"What dear?"

"You can't leave it to anyone."

"Well you wouldn't want to, would you? What would they do with it?

"And this is the breakfast room – that Aga's practically new – and through here," she opened a bright blue door, "is where we keep the old squire. You can hardly smell him at all now."

Sunlight in Spelling

Kovac kicked a pebble along the road. He was tired. He had been looking for sunlight, and there wasn't any, and he wasn't sure he'd know it if he found any. He was much too young to remember before the dust came between the earth and the sun; all the twenty-some years of his life the sky had been the colour of damp asbestos, nights as dark above ground as below it except where cities set the air alight. Daylight never stronger than it had once been on overcast winter afternoons. Some old people said they remembered sunlight, but they couldn't describe it. Yet Kovac kept wondering if the dust mightn't be thinner in places, and was always half thinking he could see sunlight just over there, and sometimes when they stopped he went to look for it.

He headed back to the truck. The headlights were on, they were always on, but that was no problem; under the hood was a fire-rock the size of a man's fist with nothing to do but run a truck, its radio and head- and tail-lights, a rock that size would last at least twelve years. Some people said fire-rocks were a miracle. Kovac didn't believe in miracles.

Donovan was asleep in the cab. The woman, Madlin, who had ridden with them from Crystelina, was sitting in the dust beside the truck, eating a mango, nibbling the slippery flesh off the skin, yellow juice dripping off her wrist and chin. She looked up when she heard him.

"A case bust open," she said. "Honest, it did."

He shrugged, and squatted beside her. She offered him a slice of the fruit that she cut off with a pocket knife; he waved it away. She licked her fingers and said, "Will you marry me?"

"No."

"OK."

"Why should I?"

"Because you want to."

"I don't want to."

"Then don't."

"Gimme some of that."

She gave him a slice, and he nibbled it, silently. He decided he didn't like mangoes. He broke off the piece he'd bitten, and gave the rest back to her. She looked at it.

She said, "Why does Eddie call you Palmer?"

"I went to Palmer University. I have a degree in psychology. That's how I know I'm crazy. I have to be crazy: I'm saving for a down payment on my own rig, which at the rate I'm paid will only take about thirty years. I should have it in time to retire. Of course I could get an ollasene-driven outfit, but since a rock-driven truck travels at approximately five times the maximum speed of an ollasene– let's wake up the boss, we gotta get this load delivered before you eat it all. These things aren't your cheap synthetics, you know, these are high class reproductions. They're expensive."

She giggled, and started on the last slice of mango as she stood up and said, "How'd Eddie buy this?"

"He saved his pay in the Service, and there was his extra-time money when he left."

"Weren't you in the Service?"

"No," he said shortly, and opened the door and yelled at Donovan, who woke up and yelled back.

It was coming on night, and Kovac slept till the clock said it was dawn. Then Donovan woke him, and because they were behind schedule they didn't stop for breakfast.

He drank some coffee which was worse than nothing at all, and Donovan rolled into the back of the cab and went to sleep. Kovac had nothing to do but drive and keep his eyes on the road.

The main roads were marked, sides and centre, with lines of luminescence, paint that glowed in the headlights. It had a hypnotic effect, the grey above and darker grey beneath fending off the eye, so that it was drawn always to those shining lines. He'd heard of drivers going off the road, their minds numbed by staring at the lines. As he thought of it he felt it happening, and cursed and shrugged it off quickly. He'd have to wake Eddie if he was going to get like that. He listened to the silence, and the faint hum of the wheels. It was too hot in the cab; they ought to fix the AC. He took a quick glance sideways; the woman had fallen asleep, slid over with her head against the door. Kovac wished savagely they hadn't brought her. She made him nervous; but when she'd asked he'd shrugged and told her he didn't mind, and she'd better ask Eddie, who was always glad of company, especially if it was female.

What aggravated him was that she made him feel happy, a queer lifting of the heart he'd thought was peculiar to childhood, like believing in Santa Claus, and a taste for cheap sweets, and hearing the same story every night at bedtime. He hated the world, he told himself, and that was how he liked it. Only sometimes, with Eddie asleep and nothing to see but the lines on the road, he knew he was afraid. Afraid of the dark. Dark every which way, dark outside and dark inside, dark in his eyes and dark in his head. He hated the world for being dark, for being black and grey. Life was a bitch. He said it to himself, relishing the words. She had said that, the last night in Crystelina; she'd listened to him when he was drunk and when he was sober she'd said, "You really reckon life's a bitch, don't you Pat?" Because he was sober now he'd laughed and made some fast answer. Life was a bitch, a whore, a nag, and just when you thought she loved you truly you'd find she'd been screwing your best friend; and she'd laugh in your face and walk off with all your money. Life was no good. And he laughed himself at his sentimentality. No-one knew he felt that way. He was always cool, laid back, have a laugh, no worries, man. Only this woman saw right through it, saw clearer than he had himself. And when she'd said it she'd asked him to marry her, and said she wouldn't sleep with him again unless he did; but she wouldn't let him leave her behind. She was crazy but he wasn't going to love her. For what? She wasn't beautiful, she wasn't pretty, she wasn't elegant, she wasn't sweet; she wasn't the good housewife and mother type. She didn't need looking after. She had no class, no reserve. She was loving and easy, and hot as a fire-forest, but you wanted more than that for marriage. She was good to talk to, but so what, so was Eddie. She wasn't even rich. He had enough problems – following the white lines, looking for something, or running from something, it didn't make much difference. Madlin was just a damn nuisance.

The thought of her name startled him, and he looked at her again. Funny thing: most people looked younger asleep, but she looked older, hundreds of years old. And helpless. That scared him, and he reached over an arm and shook her awake. She woke slowly, with a kind of groan, and she took the hand he had carelessly left on her shoulder and kissed it. He snatched the hand away.

"Chrissake," he snapped, "leave it, can't you?"

"Sorry," she said, but didn't sound it.

She sat up, yawning, and pushed back the long dark

hair, cinnamon coloured with dust; more out of habit, he thought – he realised he was watching her from the corner of his eye, and refocused on the road.

She said, "Where are we?"

"Should make Spelling in a couple hours."

"That's by the fire-forest?"

"Yeah. I've never been there. You seen a fire-forest?"

"Sure."

"Is it light?"

"Yeah."

"Like sunlight?"

"In a way I guess. So is an ollasene lamp. In a way."

"So what's it like?"

"A fire-forest?"

"Sunlight."

"It's like ... water, like glass ... like champagne – like love. Only it isn't."

"That's very clear and informative. Thank you."

"It's like itself. Suppose I say, what's love like?"

"Love's like something you see when you've drunk half a gallon more lightning that the human frame can stand."

"You know what I mean."

"Where've you seen sunlight, anyway?"

"A long time ago. I'm very old."

"What the hell. What are you anyway?"

"Whatever you like to call it. I don't know a word you'd know for it. Not human."

But that didn't scare him. He felt he'd known it all along.

He said, "How old?"

She thought for a minute. "A hundred-and-sixty-three."

"You don't look it."

She laughed. She said, "Pat, what's the world done to you?"

He was silent a long time. Then he said, "It's dark. You know Eddie, he was married once, but she left him, account of the trucking, never seeing him. But he's happy. Some people, I guess, are just like that."

"He doesn't have a degree in psychology."

"So he doesn't know he's crazy. You see this white line? I'm following it till I get to the end, and it doesn't have an end."

"What was she like?"

"I'll tell you some day – no. There were a dozen of them. It wasn't them, anyway, it was me.

"What'd I ever do to the sun, that it should go away before I was even born?"

"You've got an obsession about sunlight."

"Who's the psychologist, you or me?"

"It isn't anything, is it? I mean it's everything."

"You're being very lucid today."

"I'm always very lucid."

"You're damn boring."

That shut her up, and she gazed out of the windscreen till he apologised.

She shrugged. "I guess maybe I am. If you're bored, I must be boring."

"What was it like, a hundred years ago?"

"Light. More people. Bigger cities. Real food, almost nothing synthesised – well, no, but there was always real stuff; you didn't have to eat the synthetics. It might've been lousy sometimes, but it was real. Cooler a lot of the time – the weather, not the food. Whole different weather. Kept changing. More autos, more people moving about. People did a lot of living outside. Things grew. Plants. Everywhere. People played sports a lot. And animals –

whole lot of animals. Horses. I ain't ridden a horse in ... don't know how long. Green trees. And you could breathe air that smelt like air. Some places. Smelt like sunlight—

"And the world was run by lawyers instead of psychologists."

"What'd the trucks run on?"

"Gasoline, I guess – some kind of oil. I dunno really – I didn't have that much to do with trucks then."

"You should've kept that up."

She was quiet again, and he knew she was hurt, and was angry at her for it.

Then she said, "Hell, I had to get out of that lousy town somehow," and it was all right again.

Presently he said, "What the heck's that?"

"What?"

"Up ahead. The sky, it's ... red."

"That'll be the fire-forest," she said.

The grey above grew pinker to a crimson horizon, which glowed without seeming to give off any light. Low down, a vague, sooty blackness stood out against it. The glow grew brighter, and the blackness resolved itself into buildings. As they reached the outskirts of Spelling, Donovan woke up.

*

Spelling was a harlequin of red light and black shadow, spangling its squalid streets with glamour. The air smelled of heat, of hot bricks, hot stone, paper crisping at the edge. There was a dusting of soot on the buildings.

When the truck was unloaded, Kovac left Donovan getting papers signed and walked over to where Madlin was standing. "You still here?"

She shrugged. "Guess I am."

"We'll be finished soon; the load we're picking up won't be ready till tomorrow, so we're stuck till then.

Eddie's got a girl here; he's going to see if she's got a friend."

He let her look away, and begin to wander off, then he said, "But she probably hasn't, so how about some lunch – or breakfast, or whatever."

She turned back, half smiling, and followed him out of the yard.

*

After they ate, Donovan said, "You two coming?" and Kovac shrugged. So Madlin accompanied them to the bar where Donovan's girlfriend worked. She was small and plump and bleached blonde and her name was Betsy and she laughed a lot. Business was slack; the four of them sat at a table with some other truckers. Kovac drank synthetic vodka and ignored Madlin, except for glancing at her sometimes when he thought she wasn't looking. Her mouth's too large, he thought, she's ugly really. He was afraid he was thinking too much, and intended to drink till he stopped thinking; but he found the more he drank he more he thought. He lost track of the conversation, and he heard Madlin saying something that didn't seem to make sense, and it irritated him intolerably. He turned and hit her on the mouth. Everyone abruptly stopped talking. She licked her lip, slowly, and a thin line of blood appeared. He didn't look at her eyes. She got up, walked out of the bar; people awkwardly began talking again. Kovac didn't drink any more but sat staring into his glass. The others gradually drew into a circle that left him alone.

Presently a well-dressed young man – rather too smart, conspicuous among the jeans and work shirts in the bar – walked over and sat beside him, and said, "You look like you lost something, friend."

Kovac looked at him without expression. "Sunlight," he said.

"Sunlight?" repeated the well-dressed young man. "You want sunlight? Friend, I can give it to you"

*

Madlin walked till she came to the edge of the fire-forest, where the tall pillars of smooth, dull stone stretched up to disgorge their red-orange flames into the grey sky in belches of heat, almost out of sight but tangible even at ground level. Grey ash floated down perpetually, layering thick and soft on the ground, drifting out even to where it was cool enough to stand. Now and then, somewhere in the acres of the forest, a grey-brown pillar would spit out one of those curiously glowing red-black lumps that people called fire-rocks, and paid fortunes for – though not to the men and women who ventured into the fire to collect them. And their enormous power – which the technics, deprived of other sources, had finally managed to extract from fire-rocks – was called Universal Energy. So far they hadn't found anything it couldn't do; but then, they'd hardly started yet.

Madlin walked into the burning air and leaned against a fire-tree, drawing the heat into her body and transforming it, letting it run through her being like wine. A salamander appeared, looked through and into her with its white-hot eyes, and said in a voice of hiss and crackle, "What are you doing there?"

"Thinking."

"I don't mean this minute. I mean in general. What are you doing living out there? You don't belong there; you're not human or you couldn't see me, unless you're a saint or a magician, but you don't look like it."

"No, not a saint or a magician ... or human."

"Then why? It's cold out there."

"It is – cold is cold and heat is heat, and stone really grazes your fingers. Where I come from everything's easy, it has no value. But the strain of living out here nearly kills me sometimes. Maybe you're right; maybe I should go back. Maybe I will."

*

Kovac stared suspiciously at the well-dressed young man for some time; finally he said, "How much?"

"Very reasonable, friend." The young man named a figure.

"That's a lot of money."

The young man laughed. "Sunlight doesn't come cheap, friend – I guess you wouldn't expect it to."

"Well... Well, I guess. I'll tell you now, that's about all I got on me, so if you're planning to roll me you'd better save the time for another sucker."

The young man fervently protested his innocence of such intention, and Kovac, drunk and depressed and resentful, hardly caring what happened to him, anyway, followed him out of the bar. Kovac didn't suppose for a moment that this slicker could show him sunlight, but he couldn't ignore the possibility.

Donovan yelled, "Hey, Palmer! Where you goin'?" – but there didn't seem any point in answering.

The well-dressed young man led him right out of town, away from the fire-forest, and they stopped outside a frayed, dirty, red canvas marquee, with a tired looking sign over the doorway, in red and yellow paint, that ran, "Grand Pantechnicon Bazaar". A tiny yellow ollasene lamp gave out a feeble, dusty glow on each side of the sign. Kovac squinted up at it.

"This it?" he said.

"This is it, friend," said the other. "By the way," – he held out a hand – "my name is Alexander."

Kovac touched the hand briefly. "Kovac."

Alexander waited expectantly, but Kovac left his last

name hanging on the air alone, and the other man finally smiled and said, "Fine. Well, Mr Kovac, if you'll just come this way—"

They ducked under the grimy canvas flap and walked down a narrow passage. At the end a sign to the right read "Hall of Broken Mirrors" and one to the left "Animal Museum". They turned left, went through a space full of small dead bodies, and pushed aside another sheet of canvas. The marquee appeared bigger inside than out. They came into a small room, floored with polished wood, where a middle-aged man in a long white robe sat in a canvas chair, reading a newspaper. As they entered the room he folded the paper, put it on the floor, stood up, and bowed. Alexander bowed. Kovac, taken a little aback, stood truculently upright.

"Good day, Alexander," said the man in white. "What can I do for you?"

"May I present Mr Kovac," said Alexander. "Mr Kovac, this is Master Julian Bishop."

Julian Bishop bowed again; Kovac nodded briefly, feeling a fool. The conviction was growing, as he sobered up, that he was being taken for a rather obvious ride. He wished he hadn't come; dammit, it was Madlin's fault.

Alexander was saying, "Mr Kovac is looking for sunlight."

"Ah! Sunlight." Julian Bishop's face assumed a benevolent smile. "What all men seek, Mr Kovac, did they but know. We shall be delighted. Please step this way."

Kovac frowned. "Don't you want any money?"

"Please!" Bishop held up a hand, palm out, as if warding off unpleasantness. "We should not dream – only if you are completely satisfied. We have every confidence—" He left the sentence and led them through yet another doorway.

This room didn't look as if it was in a marquee at all. It was large and round and metallic, full of brilliant white light from an unseen source, and furnished like an old-fashioned laboratory, with chrome and glass and stainless steel. Kovac wondered if the fittings were genuine.

Julian Bishop said, "Please sit here, Mr Kovac, and you will find what you seek."

Kovac drew back. "How can you show me sunlight sitting in a chair indoors? Even I know you have to be outdoors to see sunlight."

Bishop only smiled, and said, "Please trust me. Unless you wish to leave – you are free to go, of course."

But then he would never know. So Kovac sat, hesitantly, in a metal and leather chair; someone was moving about behind him. He began to realise he had not sobered up as much as he thought he had when he arrived here.

Bishop's voice said, "Look up a little, Mr Kovac."

He looked up, and saw a shiny silver disc, not quite flat enough to reflect anything but light, that glowed white. Then he felt a hand on his wrist, his sleeve was rolled up; something cold touched his arm and a needle was stuck into it. He wanted to move his arm away at the first contact, he wanted to look down and say, "Stop," but all his attention was absorbed by the shining silver disc.

And the disc grew and swelled to the edges of vision, and it shrank away from the centre and became nothing but a great glowing hole, and he was drawn into it and immersed. The light surrounded him and filled him; his body was empty, hollow, nothing at all, in a universe of hot, white light. And the light was infinite, and acutely beautiful; and beside the fact that the light existed nothing else held the smallest significance – that the light should be was sufficient justification for everything. And Kovac, being part of the light, was also infinite and eternal and omnipotent and omniscient. He knew that the answer to every question he had ever thought and every problem he had ever suffered was as simple as breathing; and none of that mattered either, because the light was, and that was the whole of knowledge and desire.

He had no idea how long it was till the light faded, his body gradually came back, and the light shrank to a small shiny metal disc. Julian Bishop was standing beside him, looking benevolent and paternal.

Kovac looked at him for a long moment; then he said, "I'm not satisfied."

Bishop raised an eyebrow.

Kovac said, "That wasn't sunlight."

"In what way do you mean that?"

"It wasn't real sunlight. It was a drug. It was no more than some of the drugs I tried at college. It's a fake."

Bishop smiled gently, kindly but pained, indulgent. "Real sunlight?" he said. "My dear young man, how much reality do you want? Do you wish to be burned, to be blinded? You have experienced as much of sunlight as it is possible for human kind to stand. The sensation, the emotional euphoria, the psychological insight, the spirit-restoring vision. I don't deny you may obtain the same from other drugs – as well as from sexual orgasm, from 'falling in love', from many of the occult sciences, in some cases from killing others, even from hypnosis, or mass hysteria – or spontaneously, in certain cases of mental imbalance. But this is an extremely effective path, reliable, clean, relatively inexpensive, with no harmful long-term effects or unsocial aspects—"

"It's not what you offered." Kovac was vaguely aware that, stone sober, he would have shut up and paid and left, cursing; but the lingering drunkenness combined with the effect of the drug to make him stubborn. "You said sunlight. What the hell good's a sensation? You can stick your sensation. It's not what I'm looking for. I want sunlight. Actual, objective sunlight. Reality. I don't give two fingers for the sensation."

Bishop stared as if Kovac had sprouted an extra head, or metamorphosed into a giant cockroach. His mouth opened and shut as he groped for words, finally saying, "My dear Mr ... Kovac ... really, I – really, you cannot surely... My dear man, there's no such thing as sunlight. Surely you're aware of that. There never was."

"Never— What do you mean, never was?"

"Sunlight is a myth, a wish-fulfilment."

"What are you talking about?"

"It's a common enough phenomenon. Man's lot has always been so dismal, so filled with pain and monotony and disappointment, that he has dreamed of a golden age, some time in the past, when the world was light and cool, and plants grew wild everywhere, and people lived to a great age, and food was plentiful, and everyone was good and happy. We know the world has been terrible for as long as we can remember; but before that, we tell ourselves, it was better. It never was, Mr Kovac. It is a dream – a necessary dream, but no more."

Kovac's fuddled mind struggled with this and he grasped hold of one definite thought: "I know someone who's seen it."

Bishop smiled again. "Mr Kovac – a person may mean many things by saying they have 'seen the sun'. You mustn't try to interpret it so literally. I should like to help you if I can." Kovac had stood up and was walking towards the doorway. Bishop stepped quickly after him. "About the matter of the fee—"

Kovac kept walking. "You said if I was satisfied. I'm

not."

"Really, Mr Kovac, I hardly think we can —"

"Fuck off," snapped Kovac, and was surprised at himself. He retained some of the conditioning of a respectable upbringing; taboos on language were strong, and even among his peers he was relatively clean-mouthed. To use words like that to strangers, and his elders, still felt forbidden. He said the words again, and the act gave him enormous pleasure. Then he walked out of the room.

He knew what Bishop's help would be; he knew it all, had heard it all in college. Studied it, even. He'd heard all the arguments, and tried to ignore them; he could ignore this con artist quack, too. If he'd been sober he'd never have listened in the first place. He'd been hoping too hard – after what Madlin had said; damn her, it was all her fault. And where the hell was she now? Bishop was just another damn psychologist. Eddie was fond of saying, that's what's wrong with this country, it's run by psychologists. Kovac agreed with him. He reminded himself sharply that he didn't believe in miracles. He'd almost believed, but that was the woman and the alcohol. Damn them both.

Coming out of the marquee, into the red light that was unchanged through the night, he became aware all at once of a blinding headache and an imperative need to get rid of all the vodka he'd drunk. Around the marquee the world seemed even greyer than usual; dry, dull earth with pale fungi and lichened rocks; drab, grey, long-dead trees; no-one about. Kovac walked unsteadily to a grey tree, fumbled his trousers open and relieved himself. As he tried to fasten his belt buckle again, with unresponsive fingers, a wave of nausea and giddiness swept over him. He staggered, fell to his knees, and vomited. He stayed still for several minutes while the world settled back into place around him; then, with his mind horribly clear at last, he wiped his mouth with the back of his hand, rolled over, and lay on the ground and cried.

*

Madlin's body sat leaning against the fire-tree, her spirit spread out into the air, the ground, the forest, resting, absorbing, breathing. She felt the warm touch of one of the swirls of wind that chased each other around the fire-forest. Her spirit drew back into her body as she felt the touch of something else, and opened her eyes and said, "He's hurting. I'd better go. I don't know what good I can do him, but I can't just leave him to hurt."

The salamander was still there. "Duty the path to salvation?" it suggested, with a hiss of laughter.

"Duty is salvation. To get up and walk takes a terrible effort, but if you just lie there the muscles atrophy. And you get bedsores, as well as bored out of your mind."

"Why not go back?" teased the salamander. "To where the men are always young and lovely and sweet-smelling, and always willing?"

"He's not bad," she said, "for a human. His mouth never tastes of tobacco, and not often of liquor; he smells of sweat, but not unpleasantly. His hair's clean, and he shaves often enough. His teeth are good, he's got a flat stomach, and nice legs, and his hands and arms are beautiful. And his lovemaking is generous, and not arrogant. He's intelligent. And unhappy. And I think I love him... Those pretty men at home, they get a bit dull. Too smooth, too easy. They don't have the magic."

"You and I are supposed to be the magic."

"To them. But they're the magic to us – to me, anyway. The alongside is familiar, humans are the other world, the enchantment. But you know, I can be a rotten bitch, I don't give them a chance. I eat them, I use them up. I had a man, he was good, he was strong, he was never afraid to cry. I loved him more than anything. But I still treated him bad. It's a wonder he stood it. So long ago, and I still miss him. He was fair, too, but not so over-educated. So what do I do? Just the next thing, and the next. And so on."

She left the forest, and walked through the town, and the tramps and truckers and rock-hunters, and other driftwood that Spelling catered for, followed her with their eyes. She came to the grey trees, and knelt beside Kovac and kissed his ear, the only part of his face she could reach. He looked round at her and sat up, saying, "Hell, what a damned awful mess I must be."

"I've seen worse." She put her arms round him. "Tell me. I won't say a thing."

She was there, and he needed to talk, so he told her. She kissed the back of his neck and said, "Love. I'll show you sunlight if you want to see it. But not in this dreadful depressing place. There's a bit of a river a way over, and something very like grass."

As they stood up, he said, "Thanks."

"What for?"

"Not calling me a fool."

"You're not a fool. Nothing like one. I've met plenty." She led him to the bit of river, and stood in front of him, and said, "Look into my eyes."

He looked.

"Deeper," she said, "further back."

He looked down deep, through sixty, eighty, nearly a hundred years, and he saw sunlight, and the world transformed by it. He saw what she meant by saying it was like water, and glass, and champagne. He saw trees blowing, and animals eating grass, and men and women in fields and streets full of light. And he saw that Bishop's imitation had been a good imitation, and nothing like the original.

When at last he had looked enough, he drew his eyes back and looked again at her face, and said, "It is true, then."

"You always knew that."

They sat on the grass, and Kovac stared for a long time into the little red-brown stream, and let his fingers lie in the water that ran hot from the fire-forest. He looked back at Madlin. It made a hollow, sick feeling in his stomach. What the hell, he thought, maybe I should be a sucker all the way. He put out a tentative hand and fondled her breast. The feel of her warm under the cotton shirt made desire leap up with a suddenness that shook him. She didn't move. He bit his lip and took his hand away. Her hand followed it, touched his knee, moved in maddening slow curves up the inside of his thigh; when it reached his crotch her palm curved round and squeezed him gently.

He drew a sharp breath; he said, "I haven't said I'll marry you."

She shook her head. "That was wrong. No conditions. Pat, let's fuck. Now." She stopped suddenly and looked up, worried. He grinned. Her eyes fell. "I was afraid you wouldn't want to."

"You can see I want to."

She smiled, and her fingers worked at his half-fastened belt buckle as she said, "There are brothels in town. You could buy a woman who wouldn't make demands."

"And you could buy a man to do everything you said, but where'd be the fun in that? It'd be about as good as Bishop's sunlight."

Disposal of the Body

We drove Mother down into Sussex for the funeral. We asked Mark and Lisa if they'd like to spend the day with friends, but they said they'd rather come with us. We agreed that John would take them off somewhere while Mother and I were at the ceremony. It was a warm day, a bit muggy, but it didn't look as if it would rain. We took some sweets and crisps and cans of drink for the kids, and they wore their ordinary clothes, and John wore a dark suit and tie, and just Mother and I wore black.

We got away in good time, for once, and before we'd been driving five minutes there was a hell of a thump on the windscreen. I jumped, and Mother and the kids screamed, and we saw a pigeon had brained itself on the glass. John swore and pulled over, and got out to clear it off, but he left a little smear of blood, and it kept drawing my eye all the way there.

Anyway, the journey went smoothly after that, except Mother kept fidgeting and asking was I all right. We arrived at the house and kissed Aunt Jane and said Oh My Dear, and smiled and nodded to all the cousins we hadn't seen for donkey's years – or in John and Mark and Lisa's case not at all. Then we all got sorted into cars, and Mother went in one of the undertaker's limos – they had two, must have cost the earth – on account of being the deceased's only surviving sister, and not surprising as she was twenty years younger and he lived to eighty-nine. I was fitted in with one of the cousins so John and the kids didn't need to come to the crem at all, which was quite a way; it took us about half an hour.

I hardly knew the cousin, and I don't like trying to make conversation in cars anyway, so I looked out of the window and thought about Uncle Bert. I hadn't seen him for years, but when I was a kid, until I was eight or nine, I used to stay with him and Aunt Jane for holidays. I couldn't remember much about it. I'd recognised the house, and knew it had a back garden with a compost heap and a coal bunker at the end, and Aunt Jane had always given me Weetabix for breakfast, which I never had at home, and hated, but was too polite to say so. I couldn't even be sure of that, though; childhood memories get so muddled.

I found I was quite upset, and a few tears were running down my jaw.

The service was very brief, they had the crematorium chaplain, who'd never met Uncle Bert of course, and who gave the usual spiel about what a good chap he was, great gardener, fine husband and brother, and I found myself thinking, Rubbish, he was a mean old so and so, and vicious with it; which was odd, because I'd never thought that before.

There was a nasty smell in the chapel, varnish and flowers and cold, and when we stood up for a hymn or something I felt quite dizzy and sick and had to hang on to the seat in front, and I remembered I hadn't had any lunch. The hymn was very dreary, seemed to be all blood and innards, and Uncle Bert had been an atheist anyway. Well, I thought, if he's wrong he knows now.

The long shiny box slid through the curtains without a penn'orth of sound, and went to be incinerated, and we all filed out and milled about and looked at the flowers, and other people's flowers, and said goodbye to those who weren't coming back to the house. Uncle Bert's flowers were a poor lot really, but the next batch must have been for a young boy, there were floral arrangements in the shape of footballs and roller skates and even a rabbit, which quite upset me.

Then we all got reshuffled, and mother and I were put together in the back of a different cousin's car.

I said quietly, "I thought Jane looked awfully cheerful."

"I expect she's still numb," said Mother. "I was a complete zombie for weeks – you remember, Karen, you helped me do all the legal stuff, and sort out his clothes, and I was awfully calm and efficient, just going through the motions, and then one night I moved something on the dressing table, and there were his keys, and a little pile of change, and his season ticket, and it just hit me like a train, and I cried my eyes out for hours."

"I know," I said. "You were still crying when I came round in the morning. I can't imagine Jane crying."

"Sixty years is an awfully long time to be married to someone, even if you didn't like them."

When we got back to the house I saw our car wasn't there, and I assumed John had driven Lisa and Mark off somewhere, and overestimated how long we'd be gone; or maybe they wanted to escape the relatives. We went in and Aunt Jane said, "So kind of you to come, Karen. I'd quite have understood if you couldn't have faced it," and gave me a glass of sherry and moved on.

I chatted a bit here and there, and drank the sherry, and then got a cup of tea and a ham sandwich, and I was looking round, the way you do, to see if there was anyone I'd be sorry not to talk to, and I overheard behind me someone say, "But of course, you never saw him strangle a cat."

I slammed down my cup and plate and ran into the kitchen, and just made it to the sink before I threw up. I felt dreadfully embarrassed, and carefully washed away all the traces, and rinsed my mouth and splashed my face and washed my hands. Fortunately there was no-one in the kitchen, and no-one followed me in, but I couldn't face re-joining them straight away, so I went out through the back door, through the scullery of onions and buckets and wellington boots, into the empty garden.

I drew some deep breaths and felt better, and then strolled down past the rows of late vegetables to the end of the path. I went round the coal bunker, and there behind the compost heap was Uncle Bert's body. The chest and stomach were open, and shoals of fat yellow maggots were crawling in and out; his head had been battered till it was misshapen, and all over black blood; and the flies moving over it, and one lidless eye staring at the sky. There was a smell.

I looked at the body for a while, impassively, and then I walked back up the garden. There was blood on my fingers, but I rubbed it off.

I went round the side of the house, and saw our car in the road, and thought, Oh good, John and the children are back, and I walked between the dahlias to the front door, which was ajar for people coming and going. I pushed it open and walked into the little hall. The door of the back room was open, and I could hear voices, and I saw John standing there with a crumby plate and an empty tea-cup, and he said, "All right now?"

And I said, "Much better."

He said, "Are Tom and Jennifer still out there?"

And I said, "What?"

"Are they still in the garden?"

I said, "Who?"

"Tom and Jennifer. Are they still in the garden?" I just looked at him blankly, and he laughed – I never heard him laugh like that – and said, "The kids, Janie. They went

out with you."
    And I looked round for Mother.

Out of Season

I am writing this down because I do not understand it.

My name is Dorothy Castle. My maiden name was Littlewood. My sister Mabel was three years younger than me. I'd better start with what happened before the war.

Mabel was working as a typist, but she was always changing jobs, never stuck with anything. She was the pretty one, always had lots of boyfriends, a bit flighty – but stubborn as a mule once she made up her mind. We all took it for granted that Mabel would marry young. I was the steady one – I wasn't bad looking, but I didn't have SA like Mabel. Anyway, I didn't care much about boys and marriage; I had a good job in a department store, and I was ambitious. I wanted to have a career, and see the world. Funny how things turn out.

Mabel and I always took our holidays together when we could. We preferred to go at the end of the season, when the weather was still decent but lodgings were generally cheaper. In the early thirties – Mabel was about nineteen – we went down to a village in the west country called Combe; and we liked it so much we went back every year. It was quiet, with beautiful scenery and nice walks, and not a lot of tourists. We got to know some of the locals, and they were friendly – well, you know, people are often friendly to pretty girls! Men, that is. So it became a regular thing for us. We stopped in the pub, The White Lion, and there was a group of girls and chaps about our age that we went round with when we were down there. We generally met in the pub; everyone met in the pub.

There was George, who was tall and thin and gloomy, very pale with black hair, and his sister, Alice, who was much the same to look at but a lot livelier. There were Stan and Eddie, who were brothers, very alike, with red hair and freckles; they were very close, had that air of sharing a joke no-one else knows. And there was Jack, who was a big chap, good looking, with curly brown hair, and very much alive, if you know what I mean. And we all sort of knocked around together, but there was no pairing up – somehow, in those days, you didn't have to.

Well, one year it happened that I was ill in the summer, and we didn't get away for our holiday till late in the autumn, and we didn't have as long as usual. We'd had the first frost, but it was sunny, and it was nice to get out of town.

We went down on the Saturday, and met the boys in the pub. Alice was helping her father in the shop – he was the chemist. We chatted, catching up on the news, and I thought Stan and Eddie seemed put out at our coming down out of season. Anyway, we arranged to meet Jack at church in the morning – the others were Methodists, at least nominally, but Jack was C of E, and so were Mabel and I, so we went with Jack to the parish church.

Well, in the morning, Jack was just ahead of us coming out, and as he shook hands with the vicar, the vicar said, "I suppose you'll be going out tomorrow night?"

"That's right, vicar."

"You'd do much better to come to church."

Jack shook his head. "Church is one thing, vicar, and the horse is another. Let's keep them like that and not quarrel."

The vicar frowned and tutted but there was a queue building up, and he let Jack go, and shook my hand and Mabel's, and said it was nice to see us again, and we all moved on.

As we walked away, Mabel said to Jack, "What was that about?" and he laughed.

"Vicar keeps trying to reform us. Wants us to go to church instead of going to the pub and that. I told him, if I'm going to stop going to the pub, I may as well go to Chapel!"

We both laughed. Neither of us really thought that was what the vicar had been talking about, but we couldn't ask again. We forgot about it for a bit, but that night, as Mabel and I went off to go to bed, we said, "See you tomorrow," and Stan and Eddie looked away, sort of muttering.

Jack said, "I'm afraid we'll be busy tomorrow night, girls. We'll see you the day after."

"Oh," said Mabel, "but we've only got three more days. What a shame. What are you up to tomorrow, then?"

Jack looked away, and Stan said, "It's private," very curtly.

Jack said, "Now, Stan, 'tisn't their fault," and then he said to Mabel, "it's just a bit of nonsense the lads get up to. They don't like to have womenfolk around, or – well, strangers. It's just a bit of nonsense."

Well, George was buried in his pint pot and Alice was talking to some people on the other side of the room. Stan and Eddie were looking daggers, so we went off to bed, feeling thoroughly snubbed. Mabel seemed quite upset, so I said, "They're just like little boys with a gang. Take no notice." Still, we'd been friends with them for four or five years, and it did hurt.

So the next night we had our tea, and then sat in the saloon bar, but there was no-one there but a couple of old women, and in the end we went out for a walk. It soon got dark, and we thought we might as well have an early night. There were no men about, in the pub or anywhere.

I went to sleep, but round about midnight I woke up again. It was pretty dark, with just enough starlight that I could make out Mabel standing at the window, staring out. I sat up, and she said, "Dolly, come and look."

I went to the window. I could hear something – music – quite faint, but I couldn't see anything.

"It's gone," she said. "I saw it between two houses – but I think it's coming down here."

First we heard the music getting louder – there was a fiddle and two or three flutes or whistles, and one small drum. It was a rum little tune – just two phrases repeated over and over. I don't know much about music – it made me think of a little coil of wire, broken off short; thin, and twisty, and it seemed to stop just before it got somewhere. You found it going round your brain for days.

Well, after a bit they came in sight – the musicians – and after them the other men, just walking in time to the music. Then at the end – what we saw first was a skull, a horse's skull, about eight feet up in the air, and glowing, its eyes glowing. When it got closer, of course, you could see it was a man holding the skull on a pole, and the man and the pole hidden by a hood of black cloth that hung down to the ground; and there was a lighted candle inside the skull. But it was very eerie, and it made me feel quite queer. At first I thought there were other people following the man with the skull, but it was very dark and I couldn't be sure.

They all went off down the hill, and eventually the music faded, and we went back to bed. We didn't talk about it -- well, what was there to say?

We saw the boys, and Alice, the next day, and of course we never let on what we'd seen.

The last time we went to Combe was the summer of 1939, with the war hanging over us. George was married by then, and Alice was courting, and we hardly saw them. Stan was married too; we never met his wife, but it didn't keep him out of the pub. We never met any of their families and we weren't asked back for tea. We'd met George's wife, when they were courting, and a couple of times a girl that was going with Jack; a quiet little thing – but that never came to anything. It was queer, that summer, I felt as if I was holding my breath. Or maybe that's hindsight.

I never went back to Combe for fifty years.

*

I kept in touch with Alice; we wrote now and then, and sent Christmas cards. George was passed unfit for active service – it was his chest, I think; the other three went into the Navy. Jack was killed in the first year of the war, and Stan's ship went down in the North Sea. Eddie got back, but he moved away from Combe, and I never heard what became of him.

Mabel joined the Wrens, and I went into a munitions factory, which was where I met Albert. After the war I felt all unstrung; I wanted to hang on to something and stay put. I don't think I was in love with Bert, but he was kind, and understanding and considerate. What's that word Julie uses? Supportive. And when he asked me to marry him I said yes. I must say, I couldn't have asked for a better husband.

But Mabel, well, she got a good job after she was demobbed, and stuck to it, and she saved up money and got a little flat; but she said she didn't see how a person could get married when you never knew when the world was going to end. She still had boyfriends, but you could tell they weren't serious. I mean, *she* wasn't serious – and of course she was in her thirties by then. I was getting on for forty when I got wed – and most of her chaps were wanting to settle down, so they didn't last long. Still, she didn't seem to mind; she went abroad for holidays, which nobody did in those days. She took up things, did voluntary work, and she seemed happy enough. I suppose she didn't change more than I did, only the other way about.

In the seventies, Alice wrote that George had died of a heart attack.

I lost Bert quite a few years back, but Mabel and I seemed set to go on and get our telegrams from the queen. Then one summer Mabel start to feel bad. Just not as fit as she had been, with vague pains here and there. But by the time she'd been round the hospitals and been diagnosed, they said it was too late. Well, what they said was, they could operate, but at her age it was odds she wouldn't survive the op; or they could give her something that would make her feel awful, and that might give her another year or two. Otherwise it was a couple of months. I couldn't hardly blame her for choosing the couple of months.

So I was sitting with her in the hospital. They'd just done a whole raft of tests, and she was worn out, terribly thin and grey-looking. I said, "I hope you're not going to try and go back to the flat. I've talked to Julie and Pete" (I live with my daughter and son-in-law) "and they're happy for you to have David's room – he mostly lives in Sheffield anyway, now, and if he came home for the holidays…"

She tried to laugh. "I won't be there by the holidays, Dot."

I didn't really know what to say so I went on: "I can look after you, and if it gets too much … well, we'll see."

She smiled and nodded. "I upset that doctor, didn't I? The specialist."

"Oh well. It's his job, Mab, keeping people alive. I mean, if people don't want to be kept alive, he's out of a job, isn't he?" She laughed again.

I said, "That young doctor was sympathetic, though. The one I saw on Tuesday."

"Tuesday? Oh, yes, him. He's nice. He reminds me of … someone. If they could put me right, Dot— But they can't. And I'm too tired to hang about."

We were quiet for a minute before she said, "I'll tell you what, Dolly," (no-one's called me *Dolly* for forty years) "I'll tell you what I'd like. I'd like to go back to Combe."

"Combe! Whatever for?"

"Oh, I dunno. We had good times there, didn't we? The war took something out of me, Dot – I think that last time we were in Combe was the last time I was happy without working at it."

"Well, I suppose we could go there. If you're up to it."

I was doubtful, myself, but Mabel smiled, and looked almost herself again.

*

After a couple of weeks at home, Mabel insisted she could cope with the journey. Julie was quite shocked at the idea, but she knows when I've made up my mind. The summer was over, we were well into autumn, but it was still quite warm; and anyway, it wasn't going to make much difference in the end. I rang up The White Lion. It was a new landlady of course, a Mrs Auty. She said, "You've left it very late. I don't know if I can fit you in."

I took that for a sales pitch. I couldn't imagine people flocking to Combe at the end of October. Mrs Auty went away and then she came back and said we were lucky, a couple had just cancelled, and would I send a deposit.

So I sent her a cheque and a couple of days later we set

off. We felt rather swish taking a cab to Paddington, but Julie hates driving in London and I don't blame her, and Mabel couldn't manage the bus. And nowadays the nearest station is twenty miles from Combe, and only two buses a day, so we got a cab the other end as well.

It was getting on for evening by the time we arrived. We didn't recognise the outskirts of the village. It hadn't had any outskirts to speak of before the war, but now there was a council estate, and holiday cottages, and a new school, and a signpost to a trading estate – I mean a Retail Park. It was really quite upsetting. Yet the village itself had hardly changed at all.

Mrs Auty was a big, florid woman in her sixties, with hennaed hair and too much make-up, but she seemed pleasant enough. She called a young lad to bring our bags up to the room, which was nice. She was talking all the way upstairs, pointing out the breakfast room, apologising for the lack of a television. As she opened the door of our room she said, "They'll be playing tonight, of course, but if you want to go to bed before they've finished it shouldn't keep you awake. I've had the windows double-glazed."

I said, "Pardon?" wondering if they had floodlit football matches or something.

She said, "Double-glazed. So the music shouldn't disturb you. I thought you might want an early night after the journey."

She went into the room, and the boy brought the suitcases in, and I saw Mabel was looking bad, so I got her sat in an armchair before I said, "I'm sorry, what music? Is there a pop festival or something?"

Mrs Auty laughed. "Practising for tomorrow, of course. They always play the night before."

"Before what?" I said baldly. I was beginning to feel I

must be stupid or something.

"The Black Horse." Mrs Auty evidently thought I was threepence short. "That's what you're here for, isn't it?"

I shook my head. "No. I don't know what it is. We're here because we used to come here for holidays before the war and we, well, we wanted to come again."

"Really! Well, I'm blowed. Isn't that extraordinary you should have come today!"

I felt I could do with taking the weight off my feet, but I could hardly sit down while she was talking to me. I said, "Is it? Why's that?"

"The Black Horse! I'm sorry, only you said on the phone you knew the village, so I thought…"

"We used to come down before the war. We haven't been here for, oh, fifty years or more."

"But surely you've heard – oh well. It's an old tradition, a sort of procession I suppose. People come from all over. You'll see. It's tomorrow night. I'm not from round here myself of course, but it's ever so popular. That's why we're full."

I nodded. "I see. I'm sure it'll be very interesting." I took out a pound coin for the boy, who was hovering and Mrs A finally took herself off. Mabel had a lie down, and I sat in the chair.

Mabel said, "You know what that is."

"What?"

"The Black Horse. You know, Dot … you remember? That time we came down late in the year, when Jack – what he wouldn't talk about. The horse."

"Oh! Do you think it could be that?"

"Must be. It was this time of year. Now it's become a tourist attraction, apparently. They'd have hated that, the boys."

"Yes," I said, "I suppose they would."

*

The room had been modernised a bit. There was a hand basin in the corner instead of the old jug and basin, but there was no what they call en-suite, just a bathroom and lavatory down the hall. We rested a bit, and then went down to get some supper. It was the usual pub stuff. I had gammon, and Mabel had the plaice, with chips and peas and a lettuce leaf. Mabel ate a bit of fish and a few chips, and pushed the rest round her plate. It really brought it home to me, somehow, that she was dying; she'd always been a hearty eater, though one of those maddening people who never puts on weight.

Anyway, we had some stout, and she drank that, and then we went up to bed.

I opened the double-glazed window – thank God you could open them – and looked out. There were lots of people milling about. Most of them looked like foreigners – by that, I mean not people from Combe. They had cameras, and anoraks, and weren't going anywhere in particular. I shut the window.

I helped Mabel get to bed; she took her pills and went to sleep almost straight away. I was over-tired to sleep; I dozed and woke, and about midnight I got up and looked out the window. Some of the tourist types were still there, but now there were also a lot of people with musical instruments. They were all ages, kids of twelve or thirteen up to some even older than me; one old chap who was bent over almost double, but still playing a mouth organ. Some looked like local people, but there were all sorts there, women as well as men. I knew the tune they were playing, though, right off. That same tune as all those years ago, twisting round in my head like a bit of wire. I heard it, even through the double-glazing. I felt quite odd, excited and frightened and strange, like you do before something very special or important – like getting married, or going for a job you really, really want, or like the first time I went to meet Bert's mother. The bedroom didn't seem quite real, and I almost felt that if I looked in the mirror I'd see someone I didn't recognise. Silly to feel like that over a bit of music; still, I suppose it was just remembering, being taken back in time.

There was a kettle on the dressing table, and cups and tea-bags and so on; I made a cup of tea and got back into bed.

*

After breakfast, Mabel had her painkillers and a lie down, and then we went out and walked round the village. A lot of the shops were different, of course; Alice and George's father's chemist's was still there, with the same name, but I knew Alice had retired years ago, and moved out to one of those old people's flats, with a warden to keep an eye on you (Alice is younger than me, but she has bad arthritis.) We went into the shop, and spoke to a woman who turned out to be Alice's daughter-in-law; she gave us directions to Alice's flat. They involved a bus that ran twice a day, and quite a bit of walking.

We went back to the pub for lunch. Mabel ate a cheese roll and seemed a good bit perkier; she suggested we walk up the hill. Combe is sort of perched in a fold of a hill, that goes up quite a way behind the village, but it's not steep.

I said, "Are you sure you can manage the walk?"

"My legs are all right," she said, "and the pain's not bad today. I'd really like to go."

My legs were giving me gyp by the time we reached the top of the hill, but Mabel sat on a stone wall with a little sigh of contentment and gazed at the view. I sat beside her and took off my shoes. You could just see the sea in the distance.

Mabel said, "I came up here with Jack that summer before the war." She looked at me. "Did you know I was in love with Jack?"

"What?" I said, "Bless my soul, you never were?"

"I was though," she said. "But I was too shy to show it. No, you never knew that either. Funny, we've been so close, and never really knew each other. No, all the bright chat and larking about was just a sort of cover up. I could joke and flirt with chaps I wasn't bothered about one way or t'other, but when I really cared about someone – I couldn't say a word. One year I made up my mind I was going to try, but then he had that girlfriend – do you remember? – and I lost my nerve.

"Then that last year, with the war hanging over us, it was like waiting for the world to end. I thought, It's now or never; and then I thought, If this is the end of the world, what does it matter? I think he must have guessed. He asked me out for a walk, and we came up here. We didn't talk much; we didn't seem to need to. He kissed me. We kissed for a long time, but we didn't say anything. Then we came back down to the village, and I never saw him again. We wrote a couple of times – just chatty, not love letters. He was killed in the spring. Really, that's why I never married. I never found anyone as good as him, and I didn't want to settle for less."

All this was news to me. I wondered if Mabel wasn't embroidering a bit with hindsight. I said, "Well, he was a nice enough chap, certainly. Good looking, and good company. I always thought he might be a little bit – wild, maybe. A bit restless."

"Oh yes," she said, "but – Dot, why did you marry Bert? What made you decide he was the one you wanted?"

Well, that was a bit of a facer, too; it was so long ago.

"He was kind," I said after I'd thought about it. "Considerate. He always thought, What would I like, what would be best for me? He'd never hurt me. That was the main thing."

"Yes," she said, "that's the difference, you see. I don't mean I'd want a man that'd hurt me, or not care if he did. But that was never the *most* important thing. The most important thing is honesty. It'd have to be someone that would always tell me the truth, even if it did hurt. Someone I could rely on for the truth, always. No matter what."

I thought that might be a lot harder to live with than kindness but I didn't say so. I didn't say anything, in fact. After a bit we just went back to the pub and had some tea.

*

As soon as it started to get dark the streets became full of people, although there was nothing to see yet. Mrs Auty said the procession started outside the village at half past eleven and wound its way through the streets for a couple of hours, passing the pub about midnight.

"If I were you," she said, "I'd watch from the window of your room. You'll get a good view, and you'll be out of the crush. It gets very crowded out in the street."

The pub was packed. We ate supper quickly and Mrs Auty very kindly got someone to bring tea up to the room. Mabel was very quiet, and I asked her if the pain was bad again.

She shook her head. "No, but I'm tired. Not with walking up the hill, I mean, but just with living all these years. It's time, Dot. It's rotten for you: Mum and Dad, and Bert, and now me. But I think I'm quite glad in a way. It's time; I'm ready to go." She looked straight at me and said, "I hope it won't be too much of a nuisance for you."

I couldn't say anything. I just shook my head, and we

sat quietly for a bit. I think we both dozed. We were woken by the noise outside getting louder. We went to the window and looked out. I opened it but it was some time before we could hear the music. When it became audible the people in the street went quiet. There weren't a lot of street lamps and it was a cloudy night so it was quite dark, except for light coming from the pub, and a few of the houses. It was very different from the other time. I felt nervous, apprehensive; I wondered if it would be awful. At last the musicians came in sight. There were a lot of them, playing lots of different instruments: accordions, fiddles, drums, whistles, some guitars. And people lined the streets to watch them pass. It was a public event, a tourist attraction, but it still made my spine tingle.

The man with the horse's skull came after the musicians. I wondered if the head were lit by electricity now. After him came a whole string of people, dozens and dozens. After the "horse" passed, a lot of the spectators dispersed, and some lights went out so it was even darker. The stream of people went on and on. I saw someone who looked like George, only much fatter. Then, further on, there were a couple of men who looked very like Stan and Eddie. I thought, You get types, and I expect they're all related, anyway. I turned to Mabel but she wasn't there. I looked all round the room and then – I don't know why – I looked back. I saw Jack. It was definitely him, just the same as the last time I'd seen him. As I stared Mabel came out of the pub and crossed over to him. They laughed and hugged each other, and I called, "Mabel!" through the window. They both looked up and smiled. She blew me a kiss and then they went off, arm in arm, with all the others, moving in time to that queer little tune.

I ran downstairs as fast as I could – I hadn't run for years – and I struggled through the crowd in the bar. I heard them say, "Here, missus, what's wrong?" and Mrs Auty calling, "Mrs Castle! Are you all right?". I suppose I did look a bit strange. I made it out into the street; the procession was much further off now. I could just see some movement in the darkness and the light of the horse's head, high up. Then they turned in to a side street and I tried to run after them but my legs don't work that way any more, and by the time the light turned a second corner they gave out – my legs I mean – and that was that.

I had to sit down on a wall for a while; then I walked back to the pub. I must have looked worse coming in than going out, because no-one said anything. Mrs Auty made a movement towards me but stepped back, with a funny look. I went up to the room.

Mabel was lying on her bed, quite peaceful. She wasn't breathing, and there was no pulse. She looked happy.

I didn't cry out because people would have come and I couldn't cope with people. I just sat down beside her and wept, but not for very long.

Washing of the Waters

Tom went to the launderette after work. He'd become embarrassed about letting his mother wash his underwear. His pants and socks and t-shirts and jeans revolved; his eyes wandered to the wash in the next machine – would it be frilly knickers or children's pyjamas? It was red. He couldn't see anything except redness, with vague cloth shapes in it. Someone must be dyeing something. You weren't supposed to do that – there were notices.

Wishing he'd remembered to bring his iPod, he resorted to thumbing through an Argos catalogue someone had left on the bench. He looked up when a woman came in – youngish, very pale. She went to the next-door machine, which had stopped, opened the door and took out a shirt. It wasn't dyed. It was – still – badly blood-stained. She shook her head, and turned and looked at Tom.

His vision filled with darkness and roaring waters. His heart was a cold weight inside him, pressing on his lungs – then he was gasping for breath, and the launderette was empty, and his washing had stopped.

*

"Thomas! There's pork chops for your tea."

"Mum, I told you, I'm not in for tea. I'm going round Alison's. We're going to the pictures."

"Oh. Oh, I see." The words would've frozen a chicken.

*

And Alison's Mum—

"He's shiftless and gormless. What's wrong with

Trevor? He's got A-levels, he's going into computers."

*

They missed the start of the six-twenty showing, so they walked by the canal. There was a pigeon sitting on a bollard.

"That reminds me of my Mum."

"Don't be soft. Your Mum's not got feathers."

"Soft yourself. I mean the way it looks at me."

"Oh. Yours too."

The pigeon brooded. In its little bird mind it soared above the town, with the eagles that are the souls of airmen who flew into the sides of mountains or crashed in flames.

"...she thinks he's going to be Bill Gates or something."

"Uh. Mine doesn't want me to go out at all. Wants me to sit in front of the telly all night."

"I had this really gruesome dream last night. I was in this room full of animals, the smell was just gross, and they were all grunting and that, and then I heard you calling me, and I tried to answer, only I couldn't, and then when I got my mouth open all this really gross stuff sloshed into it, and it was blood."

"Oh, ugh. Then what happened?"

"Well, I started choking, and I woke up."

*

Two jealous hearts and their subservient minds wove a dark entangled web above the town. It stirred the murky water of the canal, to roil and heave, suck and swirl. Cloud straggled across the moon. Beneath the turbid quotidian ocean, the kraken sleeps with one eye open.

*

"That wind's cold. Let's go and get a coffee."

"All right. What's that?"

"What?"

"Who's that woman? She's looking at you; she's shaking something—"

"Where—? Bugger!"

"What?"

"My cap's blown in the canal. Hang on—"

"Oh, leave it."

"No, hang on - I can get it if I just—"

"Leave it, Tom. That woman - where's she gone? I don't like the look of her - oh leave it, for God's sake - please—"

The darkness wound about him like convolvulus, like brambles. His breath came short. He leaned out over the oily water - his foot slipped, and his arm and shoulder slipped under. The water was freezing. He gasped and then clamped his mouth shut as the water rose up to his face. Alison screamed. She had grabbed his other hand just before he slipped, but lost her grip. The water swirled up. He was falling; he grabbed for the bank as his legs sank under. The water sucked at him but Alison had got hold of his hand again, and his head was out of the water. His feet met something solid, something that rocked, likely a supermarket trolley, and rested.

With Alison's help he struggled on to the bank, gasping, on his hands and knees. Once he was out, she was angry.

"You are an idiot. Just because of a bloody cap. You might have drowned."

He took a few minutes to get his breath back. She was still glaring.

He stood up, looked at her eyes. He wanted to say, "I didn't mean to fall in. It was an accident. Don't be like that," but her eyes unnerved him. Instead he said, "I'll have to go home. They won't let me in the pictures like this."

Alison drew in her breath, as if to shout, then shut her mouth tightly, and flounced off. Tom stood and watched her go.

Despite malevolence thwarted, possession threatened, the darkness above the town wore a small double smirk of satisfaction.

Saxophony

The first time was a Saturday night. She fell asleep in front of the television, and when she woke it was three a.m., and on the screen he was playing the saxophone. Her first thought was, Oh, there's — and she realised there was no name to end the sentence. And yet she knew him. She was sure she knew him. The sax playing was impressive, low and dirty and incredibly sexy. She knew him so well; why couldn't she think who he was? The mouth and eyes reminded her a bit of Kenneth Branagh, but that wasn't it. He was a little plump, with sandy hair and a scrub of beard, and square hands with wide, flat-jointed fingers. She put the question of his identity to one side of her mind, and lost herself in the music.

She must have fallen asleep again; next thing there was a film on, in Japanese. She scanned the listings, but there was no music programme scheduled. Maybe it was a scene in a film. She'd check it out later – she needed to get to bed.

*

A few weeks later – it was a Sunday, lunchtime this time – she was walking through the city; the sun-washed streets were deserted between the office blocks, and she heard music. Guitars, fiddles, melodeons, and a saxophone. She followed the sound round a corner and there was a pub, a low, eighteenth century building, with the windows open and the bar full of musicians.

She went in and bought a drink. At first she couldn't see him; he was near the window, and silhouetted against the light. His playing was more up-tempo this time – you could dance to it. After a while someone did, a woman got up and danced a solo jig in the middle of the room. People moved back to give her space. The lively tunes went on for a couple of hours, and were followed by slower ones. Then the musicians took a break, and a few people sang.

Louise wondered if she should go up to him during the break. She'd had a few drinks by now, but still felt pretty sober. She was still thinking about it when a voice at her shoulder said, "Hi. Didn't expect to see you here," and she turned and there he was.

She said, "I happened to be passing. Didn't know you played here."

"Third Sundays, there's always a session. I come if I haven't got a gig. How you been?"

"Not bad. You?"

"Yeah, OK. Got a new house." He caught the barmaid's eye and ordered a pint, and another gin and tonic for Louise. "We're building on a new bathroom. Takes ages. You know what builders are like."

"Mm." That sounded like he was married. Oh well. She'd known him so long. Ridiculous she couldn't think of his name. They talked about builders.

The music started again, and she leaned on the bar and listened, and watched him, and after a bit she bought him another pint. She got into conversation with a tall blonde transgender woman at the bar and they talked about cricket. After the blonde woman left, Louise drank gin and listened to the music and watched him play.

He's not exactly handsome, she thought, but he's – I must be getting him mixed up with someone else. Or did I know him a long time ago? It feels as if he's a settled part of my life. Like someone you'd been married to for a long time. She laughed at herself; she decided he must remind her of someone she'd known when she was very small.

No doubt she'd met him casually at a club or somewhere. If only she could remember where.

People came and went. When she looked at the clock over the bar, she found it was late evening. The music was still going strong, perhaps with more percussion and less finesse. The atmosphere was thicker. The woman who had danced the jig spoke to him for a while, and Louise wondered if they were together, but then the dancer put on her coat and left with someone else.

Louise was thinking about the time of her last train, when he started to pack up the saxophone. She put on her coat and wondered whether to just say goodbye, or to ask if he was walking to the station. Before she decided he came over to the bar with his empty glass, and said, "Got to go. Long drive. You coming?"

"Uh – yeah. Yeah, sure."

"Got to have a word with Brian. Meet you outside in five?"

"Right."

She finished her drink, went to the ladies, and waited by the door of the bar. It was more like ten minutes but he came, with a long, square-cornered instrument case, and an improbable black trilby hat. There were white letters on the instrument case – *Steven Sandys*. I hope that's him, she thought. It didn't ring any bells.

He smiled and put his free arm round her, and they walked a couple of streets to his car, a long, low-slung two-seater. She couldn't tell the colour under the street lights. She said, "Nice car."

He laughed. "Got to have an extravagance. And it means I never have to give the band a lift anywhere." He put the instrument case in the boot. "Especially Norman. No way to get a double bass in this beast." He opened the passenger door, and handed her in with old-fashioned gallantry.

It was a long drive, and the last half-hour or more was through countryside, flat and nebulous under the moon. When he turned off the road, they seemed to be driving across a field. She didn't see the house until the car stopped, when the outlines of a wide two-storey building gradually emerged from the night. No lights showed; the house was a dark shape against the stars.

"Nice house," she said, thinking, Do I sound half-witted?

"Like I say, it's not finished." He took out a key and opened the front door, letting her go before him, bolting the door behind them.

He put down the sax, hung up their coats, and said, "Come and see the bathroom."

It was at the back of the house. The first thing she noticed, in the middle of a huge room, was a vast sunken tub of turquoise marble, glowing softly in indirect lighting from the walls. The second thing she noticed was a bat, swooping over the bath. She looked up. The room had no ceiling, and indeed no roof. A pale shape that might have been an owl passed high above.

"I did say it wasn't finished. Fancy a bath?"

She laughed. "Why not?"

*

The night was mild, and the water so warm it was comfortable despite the extreme ventilation. They made love slowly and easily, like people who know each other's bodies well. When the water cooled, he took her into the next room, and they carried on in a huge bed. Afterwards she slept with her arm around him.

She woke when he got up, rolled on to her back, and looked up, to see a sky paling with dawn. Vociferous birds greeted the morning all round. She hadn't realised that the bedroom had no roof either. It was remarkably warm.

She sat up, and saw him coming in with a cup of tea.

He said, "Sorry, I have to leave for work soon. If you want a lift to the station you'll have to get up now."

"OK." She drank the tea, and was dressed and ready by the time he appeared in a grey suit and overcoat, with the same black trilby, and a leather briefcase. They smiled at each other, and went out to the car.

The car was silver in daylight, and looked even lower than it had last night. He whistled as he drove, and dropped her at a deserted-looking railway station. He looked at his watch. "Should be a train to town in about eight minutes. There's a ticket machine – you got enough money?"

"Oh – yes thanks."

"You want the platform this side. Oh –" he took out his wallet and pulled out a card "– in case you need me."

"Thanks –"

He smiled, blew her a kiss, and drove off.

She put the card in her pocket without looking at it, and went into the station.

On the train, she examined the card, an ordinary business card, printed in black with a green logo: *Steven Sandys, Executive Manager, Industrial Processing, Glaister Albacore Bank* and an address in the city, with phone number, fax and e-mail.

She laughed to herself, thinking, He doesn't look like a bank manager; then thought, Bother, I never told him about seeing him on TV.

*

After that she didn't see him for a long time. She did send an e-mail, but got only an Out of Office auto-reply. She looked up Glaister Albacore Bank on the internet. There was nothing apparently remarkable, it was just a large merchant bank. There was no information about personnel.

She saw a number of people – actors, television presenters, people in shops – who had always reminded her of someone. Now she knew it was Steven they reminded her of, and always had.

She looked at the phone number on the card but bottled out of calling it. She didn't know what she would say if she did.

Spring should have been moving into summer, but it got colder; the sky was generally overcast. The air seemed to get dusty; everything was covered with a fine layer of dirt. The windows needed cleaning every day. There was speculation about nuclear pollution and global warming. Louise started finding it hard to get work. Thoughts of Steven faded from her mind; he became someone she had known a long time ago.

The year wore on, the weather got colder, the streets became dirtier. Buildings started to look black, like they did before the Clean Air Act. People wrote letters to the council, to the *Times*, to the government; letters to the Archbishop of Canterbury, letters to the Pope. None of them knew what to do about it. People blamed the Prime Minister, industrial pollutants and corporate bankers.

It was summer, and the temperature was still dropping and however often the streets and the buildings were cleaned, they still had a film of grime.

*

She found the business card Steven had given her.

Steven Sandys. Industrial Processing. Glaister Albacore Bank. There was the phone number. She still didn't feel she could call it. For all she knew he might not be there any more. It didn't really matter.

About a week later she got an email:

"Louise – sorry – computer crash – lost addresses – expect you realise what's going on. All hands to the pumps, eh? Can you come to the office? Any daytime. If not, mail me."

She stared at it for a long time; then she replied: "OK".

Walking from the underground station she looked up, as was her habit, at all the unexpected detail that lurks at first floor level and above, in stone, in green-glazed tile, in terracotta – flowers, foliage, faces, bearded men and beautiful women. One face, with hair and beard of leaves, leaves springing from the mouth, from the eyes, with a terrible vigour, like so many faces reminded her of Steven.

It was a huge glass building, shining, despite the lack of sun; all the windows seemed spotless. It took her a bit of an effort to walk through the doors. A uniformed man on the desk looked up.

She said, "I was hoping to see Mr Sandys. He's sort of expecting me—"

"I'll see if he's free." He turned away before she could give her name, and spoke very quietly on a telephone. When he turned back, he was smiling very slightly.

"Please go up," he said. "Seventeenth floor. The lifts are over there."

She thanked him, and went to the lifts.

The floor and far wall of the lift were of glass. As it moved silently up, she saw the ground recede, she hanging in mid air, the street outside dizzyingly far below. She looked out at trees and tall buildings sinking swiftly past her. At the seventeenth floor, she ventured her eyes downward, gazing past her feet down the shaft – and was quite glad to step out when the doors opened.

The corridor was bright and silent. She wondered how long it would take her to find the right office. None of the doors had names on, only numbers; she took out the card, to see if there was a clue, but she couldn't find one.

A door stood a little open, and she knocked. Steven's voice said, "Come in, Louise."

He was working at a computer; he turned and smiled as she pushed open the door.

"Coffee?" he said.

"Thanks."

There was a kettle boiling in the corner of the room. He filled a cafetière, and presently poured two cups of coffee.

He said, "Sit down. Sugar? Milk?"

"Yes. Both please."

"I've been waiting for you." There was a question in his voice.

"I did e-mail. Ages ago."

"Damn. So you did. Sorry. Well. Are you –" he paused, and seemed to change what he was going to say "– are you free tonight?"

"Tonight? Uh, yes."

"I've got meetings till late. Could you meet me at midnight?"

"Midnight!"

"I know. But you will, won't you?"

"Well. Where?"

"There's a little Turkish coffee bar, just round the corner, stays open all night. I'll draw you a map."

He sketched a neat map on a sheet of notepaper and talked her through it.

"OK," she said. "I should be able to find that. Do they get much trade round here in the evenings?"

"Oh, there's always people working late." The phone rang; he said, "Sorry," and answered it. The conversation was quite short; he put the phone down, and said, "I have to go out. I'll walk down with you."

"OK." She finished her coffee. Everything seemed

suddenly to be moving very fast.

They passed a couple of people in the corridor, looking purposeful in dark suits. A tall silver-haired man was in the lift when it arrived.

He smiled. "Good day, Steven. On your way to Price's?"

"That's right. Montague just called. They want it by Tuesday." He smiled, and the older man laughed, and shook his head.

"Ah well. When you're young." They reached the ground floor and the doors opened.

On the pavement Steven kissed her, fleetingly, and got into a taxi which pulled up at that moment. Louise felt suddenly invigorated, as if energy had been pumped into her. She smiled, and walked away in the opposite direction to that which the taxi had taken, and found a pub.

She drank white wine and listened to the surrounding conversations of young people with very expensive watches, talking about money, business, and all the intangible things that are supposed to make the world go round. And about drugs and sex and infidelity, to prove that even the rich are human. The personnel was constantly changing – no-one stayed long, no-one had time. No-one talked about the weather.

After her third glass of wine, Louise decided she couldn't stay there till midnight. She left and wandered around till she found a bus stop and went to the West End to a cinema. She chose an action movie, and ate popcorn and let the noise and movement wash over her. After about half an hour an actor appeared on screen who looked a lot like Steven. She hadn't been following the plot and couldn't work out the name of his character, or which side he was on. It didn't seem to matter much. At the end she hung about annoying the staff by watching the credits right through. She was not much surprised to see a credit for Glaister Albacore Bank, or a shot of someone in a black trilby playing the saxophone in a brief clip right at the end.

She looked at her watch; it was a quarter to eleven. She went back to the bus stop.

She found the coffee shop with no trouble. It was narrow and long and full of people talking in many languages; at the back was a wide screen showing a Turkish soap opera, and over the counter at the front a small screen showing Australian Rules football.

Louise bought a double espresso, and sat in a corner seat from which she could see the door; she shared the space with three young men arguing energetically in Polish. At midnight the door opened and Steven entered.

She was expecting the overcoat and the briefcase but he was wearing a rather ragged drover's coat and the trilby, and carrying the instrument case. Suddenly she thought again, Who *is* he, where do I know him from? But she couldn't ask now. When he saw her, he beckoned, and she threaded her way between chairs and tables and gesticulating women in black dresses.

As they went out, he said, "You do dance, don't you? I've seen you dance."

"Dance? Yes. I haven't—"

He turned and looked at her.

"—I haven't done much dancing lately."

"That's all right. You don't forget how."

The silent, lamp-lit streets were a sharp contrast to the clamour of the café. The air smelt of frost despite the season. They walked between the high, formal buildings back to the bank; Steven swiped a card to open a side door and they entered a corridor dimly lit by a blue glow from the floor. He led her to the glass lift and they rode up in darkness to the twenty-second floor, then climbed a short flight of concrete steps to another door on to the roof. It was cold, and the moon and stars very bright, far brighter than they should have been over the lighted city, far brighter than anything had been for such a long season, burning like fireworks in the clear sky.

She said, "Wow!" looking out over the vast stretch of buildings, the river a dull silver through the centre. Steven smiled, and opened the instrument case.

When he started to play, the first notes raised gooseflesh. Her blood tingled; the music got into her feet and they started to move. She was dancing without thinking about it. She moved to the music across the roof, following Steven, who was dancing too, and playing at the same time. The tune was wild but controlled, a wailing cascade of notes over a steady rhythm. There seemed to be movement around them, at the edges of her vision, but as she whirled and zigzagged she could spare no attention for it.

They reached the edge of the roof, and there was a bridge, or a ladder, leading out into the dark. She followed him over it and they stepped on to another roof, and so they went on, across town, from roof to roof, playing and dancing, coming down sometimes to ground level and then climbing again, the music curling and spinning and her feet following it. She didn't always know how she got from one place to another, or what was under her feet, but wherever Steven went, blowing the raunchy, intoxicating notes like a heady cocktail in a very louche nightclub, a solid, shining surface stretched out before and behind his jigging, reel-stepping boots. As they crossed a viaduct, she suddenly saw the heavy Victorian ironwork disappear in an uprush of – greenery. And as she spun she looked behind and greenery was following them, *that* was the movement at the corner of her eye – leaves, bushes, ivy, creepers and even trees, springing up where they passed, where their feet stirred the ground. They moved on, along the streets – still deserted though they were long out of the business district. There should have been people, but not so much as one homeless man or woman in a doorway; no cars, no signs of humanity at all, but only the riot of plant life following them. It was getting warm; sweat poured down her face and body, and not just with the dancing – the air was warm, at least as warm as it should have been at this time of the year and of the night, and it smelled of dust and sunlight.

Now the sky was beginning to lighten. Dawn was inching up in the east, and as the sun finally burst above the tallest building, the music stopped on a long growling note, and Louise stopped dancing, and they were standing by Steven's car.

*

She must have slept; she was tired beyond belief. When she woke, the sun was pouring down on her from a deep blue sky as she lay in Steven's bed.

"The summer's back," he said. "It should be all right now."

He was standing by an open window. When he turned she saw him in the light and she laughed, remembering last night and, at last, the many times before.

"Yes," she said, "all right now."

Looking Glass

It was so unfair – I *adored* Hannah. I was devastated when she died. Susan – her sister – had never liked me; I think she was jealous. I was something of a catch, if I say so myself. But Hannah loved me. Susan was just after my money, I'm sure. And she had the nerve to suggest I was after *Hannah's* money. It was so unfair.

After the funeral, I had a bit of a breakdown. Hannah had been my whole focus for so long. I just couldn't believe I'd never see her again. I had to reinvent my whole life. I saw a therapist for a while, and then I went abroad for six months and I began to feel I might live again. I'd never marry again, but life might one day be bearable.

I returned home in the middle of October and a few days later Susan rang. She apologised for her attitude before and said she realised now that I really had loved Hannah. She asked if I'd like to go to a party she was having for Hallowe'en. I didn't really want to but I didn't want it to look as if I were rejecting her apology, so I said I'd go.

It was a filthy night, wet, and blowing a gale, but I'd made up my mind, so I got the car out. I wasn't intending to drink; I don't like to get out of control with strangers. It wasn't a big party, just a dozen or so, close friends and family of Susan's, most of whom I'd met. There were red drinks – blood, you see – and nibbles shaped like bats and pumpkins, and a rather crude Jack-o'-Lantern. Susan got us playing seasonal games, most of which I managed to avoid – I really don't enjoy the indignity of bobbing for apples.

People kept talking about Hannah, which I found hard to take. Someone mentioned the inquest, and then shut up when they realised I could hear. I began to wonder whether Susan's apology had been for real. She'd said some very unpleasant things at the funeral...

The house was too hot, and I was feeling rather sick. I didn't want to eat anything; I drank half a glass of red wine, which made me feel worse. I decided to leave, but Susan said, No, no, everyone must stay till midnight. Then one of her friends backed me into a corner, telling me about some new philosophy she espoused, and I was trapped.

Susan has rather overblown ideas of interior decoration, and one wall of her living room is a gigantic mirror – God knows what it cost. It's very unnerving – it does make the room look bigger, of course, but you keep trying to walk into it. I suppose you get used to it, but even now I never have. I keep checking that what I see in the mirror is the same as what is outside it.

The multiple replication of all the orange and black decorations was nightmarish.

About half-past eleven Susan lit a huge bank of candles and turned out the lights. Then she told us that all those who were not married or in a relationship were going to sit in front of the mirror, and at midnight we would see the face of our future partner. I thought, frankly, it was in pretty bad taste to ask me to take part but she wouldn't take no for an answer. In the end I gave in. Besides me, there were two girls, an elderly widow, a divorced man in his forties, and someone's teenage son. The girls were giggly, the boy was intensely embarrassed; the other two were resigned as I was. Susan's rather forceful.

Susan lined up six chairs in front of the mirror. I wondered what she had in mind, whether she'd rigged up something, some kind of back projection, so that we'd see something. I wondered why she was so insistent on my doing it. She told us that our future beloved's face would appear behind our left shoulder – and if we were destined to die unmarried, we would see a skull or the figure of death. She got us to repeat a rhyme, some rigmarole asking the mirror to show us our fate – I can't remember it all. Then the clock started to strike midnight.

*

I don't know if the others saw anything; I don't know if Susan had set anything up. I'm sure my reaction must have been all she could have hoped for, though. I saw the mirror mist over, and I thought the candles guttered behind me, because it got very dark. And then there was a very pale, sickly light shining in the mirror, and as the mist cleared it showed a woman's face – the skin drawn tight on the skull, but still recognisable – and she smiled, and beckoned to me, with a very white hand, in which you could see the bones. I thought for a moment my heart would stop. And then everything misted over and the next thing I knew one of Susan's in-laws was gripping my shoulders, encouraging me to put my head between my knees.

I got away soon after. I don't know if it's any satisfaction to Susan, but I feel I haven't got long left. The woman in the mirror is still in front of my eyes, beckoning with that skeletal hand. No, it wasn't Hannah. I told you, I adored her; I shouldn't be afraid of Hannah. No, it was Emma – my first wife – the one with the money. The one I murdered in order to marry Hannah.

She keeps beckoning. Sooner or later I'll have to go.

Christmas Present

Doris heard the slight *plip* of the cat flap, followed by the *scrutch scrutch* of claws at work in the doormat. There was a pause, then the *plink* of the name tag on a collar against the rim of the food bowl. After a while she heard the claws in the carpet behind the sofa, a pause, and the air was enriched by the fishy aroma of a well-timed feline fart. Doris smiled and shook her head. She must start tidying the house – it would be Christmas Eve tomorrow, and Norman and Christine would be round early.

Doris wondered where she had gone wrong with Norman. He wasn't a bad son; but one of the things that were immutable in Doris's universe was that you didn't leave your old mother all on her own at Christmas. They would come round, exchange presents, have a drink and a mince pie, and then move on. Perhaps it was her fault to some extent ... when the children had come to Norman's for Christmas, Doris had joined them – it wasn't far. But then Catherine had married, and the family centre of gravity had moved with her to Nottingham. That meant at least two nights away, and Doris had demurred at leaving Charlie. The next year Doris had hinted heavily that they should all come to her, but they had said, Oh no, it would be too much work for her, and Norman had pointed out that the bungalow wasn't big enough for the Nottingham contingent to stay. Doris was sure they'd have managed somehow. But after all, Catherine had the new house, and then next year she had the baby... Still, thought Doris, they didn't have to stop asking her, even if they thought she'd say no. She sighed. She didn't, in all honesty, really mind being on her own, but it was the principle of the thing...

*

The bungalow was spotless by the time Norman and Christine arrived (Doris heard the outbound *flup* of the cat flap as the car drew up). They brought in two big bags of brightly wrapped parcels, ceremonially exchanged them for one biggish bag from Doris, and then sat down, at her insistence, while she made tea and coffee. She knew Norman would have preferred whisky, but Christine insisted he share the driving. Doris liked Christine, they understood one another. How she put up with Norman all these years...

There was a plate full of home made mince pies, and some biscuits shaped like Christmas trees that Doris had bought at the church bazaar.

Doris said, "You shouldn't have got me all those presents, it's very sweet of you, but it's very naughty, spending money on an old woman like me."

This was meant to provoke a protest that they couldn't do enough for her, that Christmas presents in abundance were the least they could offer, but Norman just said, "They're not all from us of course. Catherine gave us theirs when we were up there three weeks ago, and Stuart came down from Leeds on Tuesday, so there's his as well. And a couple from Mrs Abernethy next door."

"That's nice of her."

"I think she's starting to fail, her memory's going."

Christine put in hastily, "She's always had a soft spot for you, Doris. Always asks after you when I see her."

"I must give her a ring."

Norman said, "She asked after Charlie the other day. You know, Mother, Christine wouldn't let me get the present I wanted for you, but I do wish you'd think about it."

"Norman! I wish you'd stop. When Doris is ready for a kitten, she'll say so."

"Oh!" This had come up before, but Doris wasn't expecting it now. "Yes," she said, "yes, I'm not sure about a kitten."

"Look, mother, I know you always said they wouldn't get on, but—"

"Well, you know, I think a kitten might be a bit too much work. I'm not as spry as I was."

"Perhaps an older cat, then? Or a budgie, or something? You need company."

"Not a budgie... All right, Norman, I'll think about it. Really I will."

Norman was beginning to look stubborn, as he did when he was sure he knew what was good for you, and Christine hurried to turn the conversation, via a mince pie, towards cooking, for which Doris was thankful. She didn't want to have to talk about kittens, or budgies. Obviously, Norman couldn't understand, but a more sensitive person would pick up that she didn't want to talk about it, and leave it at that. Oh well. He did take after his father, but without her late husband's saving grace of wit...

They each had one mince pie and one biscuit, gently but firmly refused a second drink, and said, Well, well, we'd better get on. She saw them off, poured herself another cup of tea, and looked at the bag of presents. There was a card from Mrs Abernethy, and two small parcels. She opened the card, put it on the mantelpiece, and examined the parcels. One was addressed to her, and was obviously talc; the other was addressed to Charlie, and was probably a catnip mouse ... she hadn't seen Mrs Abernethy for months. She must ring her. Dear, dear. She felt quite tired; Norman often had that effect on her. She had another mince pie. They really were rather good.

Yes. A kitten or a budgie. Goodness knows. It *might* be perfectly all right, but... On the one hand, the kitten or the budgie might get the fright of its life. On the other, they might drive Charlie away, and she wasn't quite ready for that yet. But there was no way to explain to Norman. She wasn't ready to be put in a home either.

The cat flap *plipped,* and she heard the claws in the mat. She reached for another mince pie and settled back on the sofa. In a minute or two she heard a soft landing on the sofa and felt, but did not see, Charlie settling down on her lap. She wrinkled her nose. Who would have guessed, she thought, that a ghost could still fart.

Overnight Bus

By one a.m. the bus that had been due at ten-thirty p.m. still hadn't arrived. There had been a couple of announcements, to the effect that the ten-thirty service to Kimberley had been delayed, but no suggestion of by how much, or indeed that the announcer knew any more than the rest of us. Most of the passengers seemed resigned to an indefinite or even infinite wait – they sat around, eating biltong and roasted mealies, talking, sleeping on the wide wooden benches, with cases, with paper parcels, with huge laundry bags of luggage, with sleepy toddlers and fretful or somnolent babies; the air was hot, heavy and thick. A few obvious tourists slept against rucksacks in a corner.

The excitement I still felt simply at being in Africa was fighting against the need for sleep, and a feeling in the pit of my stomach that the bus might never come, which emphasised horribly the pointless and ludicrous nature of my whole journey. I should have given up this silly plan, and stayed with Anne's aunt in Jo'burg, or maybe gone to Cape Town for a few days as she suggested. Which would also have involved a long time on a bus, but at least with a goal I wasn't embarrassed to mention.

There was a queue at the counter, where the Indian clerk had been checking someone's ticket for at least five minutes, typing things into his computer terminal, looking back and forth between the screen and the piece of paper with a frown, and scribbling notes. There were six people behind the man with the disputed ticket, and I decided I didn't have the stamina to queue. Ian's face came into my head, but at the moment it was just a face, hardly more meaningful than any other. Hardly worth queuing for.

But I was here now. I curled up next to my bag and dozed for a bit; I was woken by another announcement telling me the coach to Kimberley was delayed. The queue was shorter now, and the clerk had gained reinforcements. I stood up and joined the line, and fairly soon was talking to a young African man with a wide smile and a very soft voice.

I said, "Do you have any idea when the bus to Kimberley will be here?"

"The bus to Kimberley is delayed."

"Yes, I know. It should have been here three hours ago. Do you know what has happened to it?"

He shook his head. "We know it left the last stop one hour late. We have not heard since then. It may have broken down."

"You haven't heard anything at all?"

"No. The driver should have a cellphone, but it may not be working."

"So, if it doesn't get here at all, how can I get to Kimberley?"

"There is another bus at ten-thirty in the evening."

"You mean there's only one bus each day?"

"That bus, yes, it runs once a day. There is another bus, which will leave at two-thirty, in one hour, but it is a local bus."

"A local bus? Where does it go?"

"It goes to Kimberley."

"So – sorry – what do you mean when you say it's a local bus?"

"It is for local people – not for tourists – it will not have the same facilities."

"Such as what?"

"There will not be any entertainment, and there will not be food or drink served."

"Will there be a toilet?"

"Yes, there will be a toilet."

It was two in the morning. I didn't want food or drink or in-flight movies. I said, "Can I use this ticket for that bus?"

He took the ticket and checked various things on his computer screen. "Yes," he said, "I can change this ticket so you can use it for the local bus. You are sure you want to do this?"

"Yes," I said, "I do want to." The thought of another eighteen hours in this bus station was not enticing. The seats were only comfortable for a fairly limited time, and there were strongish smells of people and food, and some of the babies seemed to need their nappies changing.

I said, "Is there any difference in the price?"

He shook his head. "I cannot refund any money. You understand there is a charge for changing the ticket?"

"How much is that?"

"You will not pay any more, you will not pay that. But I cannot refund. Yes? You understand?"

"OK. But – OK, that's fine." I was slightly puzzled by his insistence on no refund, when I had in fact been expecting an extra charge.

He gave me a new ticket and I trailed off with my suitcase-on-wheels to look for stand 174F. The coach was loading by the time I arrived – I'd been half afraid it might be one of the peeling, rusty, highly unroadworthy-looking vehicles I'd seen a few times at the side of the road, apparently broken down, with luggage on the roof and resigned passengers sitting about on the ground. But this looked in good repair, just like the other "tourist" coaches I'd travelled on. The driver put my case in the luggage compartment and I climbed up with my shoulder-bag and looked for my seat.

I saw then why the clerk had thought I might want a refund. The bus was about the same width as usual, but instead of two seats either side of the aisle there were three; the leg-room was pretty limited too. I was the only white person on the bus, but I was getting used to that. I had a window seat, which was a bit of a pain, since it was pitch dark and nothing to see, and it made it difficult to get up if I wanted to go to the loo. Anyway, I would be moving, so it was better than more hours in the bus station.

It took a while to get everyone on but eventually we started, and gradually I relaxed and felt again how dreadfully tired I was. The people beside me were talking, but no-one was speaking English so it was quite easy to tune it out. The bus was a hive of activity, people eating, drinking, nursing babies, changing nappies; I heard an odd noise, and after craning round a few times I realised someone a few rows behind me had two chickens in a box. It wouldn't have surprised me if they'd had goats as well – perhaps not cattle, the bus was too small – but I couldn't see any. The smells of the food and the nappy changing made me slightly queasy; I found the bottle of water in my bag and drank a little.

After half an hour or so the driver dimmed the lights and the noise died down a bit, and I started to doze. I was vaguely aware of movement in the near darkness. People went up and down the aisle; once I almost thought someone *had* brought a goat on, there seemed to be something going past that wasn't a person, but I was too sleepy to take much notice.

I thought, sleepily, about why I was here and how stupid it was. OK, the holiday had been a good idea, get away from the English winter, see new places, meet new people; but a long cross-country journey, to a place where the main attraction is a hole in the ground, to see someone who really wouldn't be pleased to see me...

The woman beside me tapped my arm and said something, thrusting a plastic box in front of me; it took a moment to realise she was offering me whatever was in the box, presumably food. I blinked, and shook my head, and said No, thank you; but she insisted, saying, "Please, please," and eventually I took a brown lump of something, smiled and said Thank you, and ate it, rather dubiously. It turned out to be chicken cooked in spices. I hoped desperately it wouldn't disagree with me.

I'd met Ian at a party, and we'd snogged a bit, probably because he couldn't find anyone better; and that should have been that, and would have been, except that a couple of weeks later I saw him playing in a county cricket match, and fell violently in love with him. How stupid is that? He was averagely pleased to see me, but no more; by the end of the season it was blindingly clear he was never going to return my feelings. When I discovered he was going on an England A Team tour of South Africa for three months, the thought of his being on a different continent for so long was unbearable. Go figure – what difference does it make if someone's in Kimberley or Canterbury, if they don't see you? But it mattered. I had no money, of course; I wangled an invitation to visit the aunt of a South African colleague at work, who lived in Sandton, and I scraped and borrowed enough for the flight and a bit of a tour round. The aunt was astonishingly hospitable. I felt a bit guilty, although I was paying something for my keep, and had taken out a load of stuff my friend didn't want to trust to the post.

The woman beside me was now offering me a drink

from a bottle of orange squash. I was even more reluctant to accept but could think of absolutely no polite way to refuse. I took a sip, trying rather absurdly not to let the bottle touch my lips, wiped the rim and handed it back with more thanks.

So, I had been to a couple of tourist sights and had spent a good deal of the week on buses; I didn't feel I could just go straight to the match, with no further explanation. Despite the embarrassment, though, I was utterly determined to go through with it. How Ian would react when he saw me, I didn't even want to think.

I slept for a bit, with horrible dreams of trying to get to Ian on the other side of the road, but being prevented by the huge stream of people and goats – huge goats – that was flowing between us. I woke up when the coach stopped, the lights went on, and everyone started talking again, and getting up and taking down luggage and gathering up babies and disembarking. I didn't think we'd been on the road long enough to reach our destination – it was still pitch dark – but I got up and moved dozily to the front. The driver said, "We stop here, madam, for one hour. Make sure you are back before we leave."

I nodded and said Thank you, and climbed down.

It was much less hot now, and the air smelt fresh. We had stopped in a large open courtyard, with low buildings around, and a great high building along one side. There were many tables and chairs and benches, and people seemed to be fetching food and drink from some of the low buildings, and sitting down. I wondered what time it was, but my phone had switched itself off and when I switched it back on it wanted *me* to tell *it* the time. Whatever, the middle of the night seemed a funny time to start eating and drinking, but I thought maybe the bus company had to have a break in any journey of more than a certain number of hours.

I wasn't hungry, so I just sat down at one of the tables. There were dim lights in some of the buildings, and open fires here and there in the courtyard, but it was still tremendously dark; outside the circles of light I couldn't make out people's faces until they were close up. Perhaps because I was still the only white person there, people kept approaching and looking at me, smiling, shaking my hand; they didn't seem to want to talk. A small girl came and stood beside me, smiling shyly; after a little while she reached out a hand and touched my hair, first on my shoulder and then the side of my head; the feel of her tentative fingers was strange, but rather pleasant – I smiled back, and she stroked my hair a few times and moved on. A lot of the men were drinking some lethal-looking local beer from a plastic barrel; one offered me a cup, but I shook my head, and then someone else gave me a bottle of Castle, which he took the top off of by banging it against the table. I thanked him, and drank; it was quite welcome by this time, although I was afraid it would send me back to sleep.

There was tremendous milling about: people sat and ate and drank, then got up and moved about again. A woman with a baby on her back sat opposite me; she unfastened the blanket that held the baby and placed it on her knee, and then held a very animated conversation with another woman, who kept pointing across the courtyard. After a while the second woman looked at me, and said something to her friend; the mother nodded and stood up, holding the baby out to me – "Please," she said, "you hold my baby?"

"Uh – sure, OK." It seemed a fairly simple thing to ask. She put the baby on my knee, and I held it while it gazed at me with large, solemn eyes. It was pretty well wrapped up, despite the warmth of the night, and its gender was quite unguessable. The two women walked off, talking excitedly, towards the large building.

The baby seemed contented, or perhaps resigned. Perhaps it was still at that age where other people are undifferentiated, and so long as it was warm and not hungry it was quite happy. I confess to knowing little about babies. They seem to appreciate attention, though, so I jiggled it a little, and talked to it in a random stream of consciousness. "Don't know how long we're here for, baby, but I can see the bus, so if people start getting back on, I hope your mother comes back for you." I tried to check how long I had been there, but now the phone battery had suddenly died, so I made sure I was facing the bus, a looming shape against the slightly lesser darkness of the sky.

People continued to move past, some smiling at me, some talking; some, not quite close enough to see clearly, looked extremely strange. Further off, I could have sworn there were people with leopards' heads, and something like a great snake with a strangely shaped head, towering over the crowd – but I'm sure it was a trick of the dark. Possibly someone in a ceremonial headdress – there were all sorts of clothes, from jeans and tee-shirts, suits and ties, and skirts and jumpers, to robes in brightly printed cotton, animal hide loincloths, exiguous skirts of fur, one-shouldered tunics in mud-coloured fabric, to practically nothing at all. So far as I could remember, the people on the bus had been mostly in – well, what I think of as ordinary clothes, skirts or trousers and tops, or the women in sort of swathed outfits of printed fabric. There certainly weren't all these bare torsos, and I didn't remember the leopard skins either.

I finished my beer, and someone gave me another. He

grinned at me and didn't seem to want any money. I began to hope that the mother would come back before too long, as babies are astonishingly heavy after a bit. I shifted it a little on my lap, trying not to disturb it, and it murmured to itself, but didn't cry or complain, only gazed at the world wide-eyed. I was starting to feel a bit panicky – what would I do if the bus started off and I still had the baby? I could neither abandon it nor take it with me – would the driver wait while I looked for the mother? Could I hand it to somebody else? Perhaps she wasn't coming back, perhaps this was a way of divesting herself of a baby she couldn't afford to feed... And what was going on here, anyway? Who were all these odd-looking people? Fear of the unknown, which had been subdued by adrenaline for a week, surfaced through my tiredness and flared in my head. If this were a book or a film, I would be on the look out for the hidden agenda, the food and drink would be drugged, or designed to fatten me up for sacrifice to strange gods – and weren't those strange gods I could see in the dark, that great serpent –? Was this some ceremony that outsiders might not witness and live? Or, was I to be the victim of a more mundane plot, robbed and murdered for my money and passport, maybe raped first? The baby grunted and wriggled, bringing me back to the actual, and I took the weight on one arm while I checked that my wallet was still in my bag, and my passport in my pocket. Of course, it could be that I would simply have to spend eternity in this courtyard, the bus would never leave, the sun would never rise... I used to have feelings like that often as a teenager. Once I remember coming back from the loo at a party and wondering if everyone would have vanished while I was gone...

People were still smiling at me, and shouting

incomprehensible greetings. Someone put a small bowl in front of me with maize porridge and a dollop of tomato and onion relish, and encouraged me to eat; I thanked her and rearranged the baby so that I had a hand free. I pressed down the thought of the food's being drugged, or fattening me for sacrifice, but I still hesitated, not knowing where the food had come from, who had touched it. I stared at the bowl, and at last I thought, Rubbish, these people are just as clean as I am, this baby is clean, it smells clean; the food is no more likely to be dangerous here than anywhere, less so, it is all freshly cooked. I could see cooking pots on some of the fires, and people ladling stuff into bowls. I ate – messily, not being used to using my fingers so – and it was unexpectedly enjoyable and I realised I was quite hungry after all. When I had eaten I looked round to check that the bus was still there, though really it could hardly have left without my hearing it.

I became aware that there were fewer people around; the fires were still burning, the coach was still parked, but everyone was moving towards the large building on my left, at the head of the courtyard. I had registered it when I got off the bus as a two-storey concrete structure, with a couple of lighted windows. What I saw now was a great stone building, three or four storeys high, its ground floor blank but for a wide doorway, but with windows above, and both doorway and windows blazing with light. It hardly looked like electric light. If it hadn't been steady you would almost have thought the place was afire, it blazed golden against the blue-black of the sky. As I gazed around, the whole courtyard looked bigger; it stretched out on all sides, and instead of small iron or wooden huts, the space was defined by a wall, twenty feet high, immeasurably old, the light catching geometric patterns in the stonework. There seemed to be hundreds of people congregating in a wide open space in front of the tall building. They began to sing.

Suddenly I felt a lift of my heart, a great surge of joy. I was in the middle of Africa, and I could be anyone, do anything. Suppose the bus went without me? I could find my way to Kimberley, probably recover my luggage. People would help. I know some people will rape and beat and rob you and leave you for dead, but a lot more won't. Even those who don't care will often help if you nag enough, like the importunate widow in the parable. And why should the bus go without me? Meantime, here I was, not having to be any of the things that were expected of me at home, entrusted with this quite delightful baby, and I felt that even if the mother never came back the baby and I should manage somehow. I looked at all the people around with extraordinary benevolence. Some were, I supposed, by their costumes expressing kinship with leopards or buffalo or snakes – if there is such kinship, then how much more between human beings, whatever their colour or language or name for God? We are all very much more like each other than any of us is like anything else. Even Ian, just for the moment, was simply part of humanity, and I loved him no more nor less than all the rest.

I murmured some of this sudden epiphany to the baby who continued to look around with solemn amiability, and after a bit gave a deep sigh, put its thumb in its mouth, and appeared to go to sleep, resting its head against my breast.

I looked back at the crowd before the great stone building. Their singing was slow and chant-like. To begin with it sounded strange and rather eerie, but I began quite soon to tune in to its sound and received a sense of strength and purpose, increasing in intensity, as though the singing were enacting something. The singers began to move in a slow, shuffling, very rhythmic dance, with hand clapping, hypnotic, compelling. It was scary and exciting. I chose to go with the excitement. Though I was more or less immobilised by the baby I felt drawn in, as though somehow my energy was contributing to whatever action was being performed. At first this terrified me, but as it built up the energy that filled me became irresistibly positive, a surge of goodwill towards the whole world – OK, it sounds corny, but I really felt as if I were connected to the whole human race, and could affect it for good or ill.

As I watched, the light in the building grew, and another light rose behind it, like sunrise, except I was pretty sure that wasn't the east. A great figure rose against the light – far too tall for anything human. It looked like a huge snake with the head of a fish – but silhouetted against the light it could easily have been an illusion. In front of it, people with the heads of leopards, lions, buffalo, hippo, rhino, giraffe, elephants ... danced and sang in a semi-circle. The energy rose from them, from the great snake, rose like a sunrise behind the building. Whatever was intended seemed certain of effect; my feet moved in rhythm with the singing, shuffling so as not to disturb the baby; my hand moved too, on the table.

The baby stirred and mumbled. I looked at it and jiggled and murmured; and abruptly the light diminished. When I looked up the sky was dark and only subdued gold lights burned in the windows of the great stone building. The singing died away and people began drifting back towards me.

I finished my beer and soon the baby's mother appeared. It woke, blinked up at her, and held up its arms, and I surrendered it, to beams and thanks and enthusiastic handshaking. Her friend helped the mother strap the baby to her back, and they wandered off. I saw the driver get on the bus, and switch on its lights. I stood – rather stiffly – and made my way back. In a few minutes, everyone was in their seats – still no goats, but I'm sure I heard something bark at the back.

The bus's lights remained bright for a while. The woman next to me was reading an English language magazine. I glanced at it; a subhead in a story or article caught my eye: "No Love is Ever Wasted". I wondered vaguely what the story was about. I also wondered what the time could be; surely it should be dawn by now but the view out of the window was still of blackness. I was suddenly intolerably sleepy – no doubt the beer had a contributory effect. I drifted off and slept till we stopped, in the beginnings of dawn, at another bus station – Kimberley, this time.

I struggled off, retrieved my luggage, and found a taxi to take me to the cheap hotel I'd booked by phone. The memory of the night stop was fading but I was sure it wasn't a dream. Still I didn't have much attention to spare for it now: I had something of a job conversing with the Lithuanian taxi driver; and then when we arrived at the hotel they admitted I'd made a reservation but said they had me down for the following week, and sorry, they were fully booked. I complained vigorously, waved my arms a lot, emphasised that I was a woman alone, with no transport and nowhere to go, and eventually they made some phone calls and said they had got me a room at another hotel, at the same price, and called me another taxi to take me there. This driver was Polish, but we managed to understand each other fairly well.

The new hotel turned out to be part of a rather classy chain, three- or four-star, and rather bland and mass-produced. I didn't take much notice, being still somewhat bleary-eyed, beyond being quite pleased at the result of the arm waving and stroppiness. When I had checked in, deposited my luggage, washed my face, and found out breakfast was still being served, I realised that I was in the same hotel as the team – there were cricket bags in the lobby – and as I entered the breakfast room I saw Ian at the far end carrying a bowl of cornflakes and a glass of orange juice back to a table full of scrubbed-looking young men.

My first reaction was delight. My second was uncertainty. How would he react to seeing me? Could I convince anyone I was here by accident? For a moment I considered returning to my room for an hour, but despite eating in the middle of the night I was craving food again, and more especially the stimulus of tea. Breakfast took precedence over not appearing a mad stalker. I was shown to a table, ordered some tea, and went to fetch porridge and juice.

While I ate I thought, What am I going to say? Should I ignore him altogether, avoid speaking to him at all? That would look weird, too. I was starting to panic now he was actually in the room: will he ignore me? Will he warn me off? He can hardly have me arrested. I can prove I didn't book into this hotel deliberately. Oh God. Why on earth did I come? I was keeping my eyes away from Ian's table but I sneaked a sideways glance: he was at the buffet putting bacon on a plate. I watched him as far as the toast machine and then looked away. I wondered if he'd seen me. The urge to go and make toast was strong but I resisted. A waitress brought my tea; I poured a cup and thought, Come on, what's the worst that could happen? He *can't* have me arrested. If he's rude to me, I've made a fool of myself, but it'll be all the same a hundred years from now. I'm having a fantastic holiday, I had an extraordinary journey last night, which would never have happened otherwise. OK, I've irritated the poor man dreadfully, but if that's the worst that ever happens to him he won't have a bad life. I felt quite brutal for a moment but, after all, it was true; God knows I've been irritated by enough unattractive men in my life, but I've survived. I'm here, eating breakfast in a four-star hotel, and if he wants I'll apologise and go away. It absolutely isn't the end of the world. I can survive, I thought, even if I never see him again.

All the time, of course, the thought of him, the knowledge that he was in the room, was filling me with a singing delight, and the effort needed to keep looking away from his table was considerable, but I managed it. Later, as I spread honey on toast, I became aware of his approaching me – I had developed a hyper-awareness of his presence over the last few months.

He said, "Hi, Alison. Didn't expect to see you here." There was wariness in the tone and uncertainty of reception, but he was obviously trying to be laid back about it.

"Hi, Ian. Yeah, kind of a last minute holiday, been staying with a friend in Jo'burg, and thought I'd come out here and watch the game."

"Oh right. Long way to come."

"Well, long way to come from London, but not so far from Jo'burg." I smiled, trying to keep it light.

"Yeah, guess so. How are you getting out to the ground, then?"

"Get a cab, I suppose."

"I'll see if anyone can give you a lift, if you like."

"That'd be cool. Thanks very much."

"See you later. Uh – nice to see you."

"You too." I smiled again, hiding the completely gobsmacked feeling, I hoped, reasonably well, and he glided away. I thought, finishing my toast, There's a thing. I went back to my room, got sorted out for the day and then went to hang around in reception. I looked at headlines on the rack of newspapers: "Breakthrough in Peace Talks", "Roep vir skietstaking", "Dictator Toppled". I looked out of the main door to where a woman was walking past with a baby on her back; she smiled and waved at me, and I smiled and waved back.

*

I drove to the ground with the team coach's Australian wife, a cheerful blonde in her fifties. She asked me the usual polite questions, and said, "So, you're not Ian's girlfriend?"

"No! Oh no, just a friend."

"It's good that you came. It's a long time away from home and the guys really like to see friends. Oh, I nearly forgot – Ian's given you one of his comp tickets, it's in my bag. Why don't you come and sit with me, unless you're meeting anyone?"

"I'm not meeting anyone, no. That'd be great."

"Be good to have another woman to talk to!"

I smiled at her and looked in my bag for sunblock. It was already hot outside, with hardly a cloud in the sky.

Indecent Behaviour

It was Thursday night. Jason's pay had run out and Lenny's giro was late, so they left the pub early. Outside the bar the cool air smelled of smoke, the pavement covered with fag ends. "What shall we do then?" said Lenny

"Not much *to* do," said Jason.

"Let's go down the late night Paki and nick some booze."

"They don't open after nine, not since the last time."

"I know – let's go down the Feathers and duff up a queer."

Jason made a face. "It's a long walk."

"Well, what then?"

"Oh all right. Might as well I suppose. There's always cops round the Feathers." Jason was a pessimist.

Lenny, who hadn't the brains to be a pessimist, laughed. "The filth won't take no notice. They're after the poofters. We'll be doing 'em a favour."

"Probably rain again."

*

They stood in a doorway across the road from the Prince of Wales Feathers, watching men come in and out in groups and couples; some wore uniform leather and chains and large moustaches, but most looked worryingly like Jason and Lenny, in t-shirts and denims or combats, some with jackets, some without, in that uncertain season between spring and summer.

Jason started to get nervous, folded a stick of gum into his mouth, and said, "Come on, this is a waste of time."

"No, hang on, there's one now. That old geezer."
"Uh. OK."

The man who came out on his own and walked briskly away from the town centre was smallish, in his sixties, with neat silver hair, very dapper in a light suit, pink shirt and cravat. He walked with small, quick steps. On the far side of the road they kept pace with him easily. Once out of sight of the pub they crossed the road, and he became aware of them. He walked faster, not quite running. The streets were deserted, lined with closed and often empty shops, small workshops, offices; half the street lamps were out. The side turnings were darker than the main road. Soon they came alongside a breaker's yard, opposite a parade of lock-up shops, half of them boarded up, all of them shut. A rat scuttled out of the yard and disappeared in the darkness.

They walked faster; Jason moved out to one side. The old man stopped under a solitary street lamp. Lenny grinned with all his teeth, like a shark, and said, "Hallo, Grandad."

*

Two weeks later, Lenny had a nasty turn in the gents at the pub, when the navvy at the next urinal put a hand on his prick. At least, Lenny thought, it must have been him; there was no-one else in there. Lenny was rather small and skinny; the navvy was six-four and built like a brick shithouse, and the look Lenny got when he said, "Oy —" shut him up. But what kept him quiet afterwards was the fact that the navvy had hands like legs of pork, sunburnt and hairy, whereas the hand Lenny had felt and seen on his privates was small, soft, white and well-manicured.

Lenny went back into the bar, a little bit shaky. After about half an hour Jason entered, looking worried, holding an evening paper. He pulled Lenny over to a corner and spoke in a hoarse whisper: "'Ere, Len. You know that old queer we done over? He died."

"Couldn't of."

"Well he bloody did."

"Must've put the boot in too hard."

Jason threw down the paper and went to the bar for a couple of pints. When he returned, Lenny said, "D'you reckon the filth'll be after us?"

Jason drank about half his pint and thought about it; in the end, pessimism lost out to practicality. "Nah," he said, "who seen us?"

"Yeah, right." Lenny grinned, cheerful again. He forgot about the nasty moment in the gents.

*

Next day, Jason got home from work feeling horny. As he banged the flat door, waking the baby, Sharon put his tea on the table and was a bit surprised to hear him say, "Never mind the tea, get 'em off."

"What?"

"You heard, get your pants off."

Bugger, she thought, now he'll complain the tea's cold. She took off her skirt, tights and knickers. He was more impatient than usual, shoving her hard on the couch and flinging himself on top of her – and all at once the prick pushing at her thigh went soft as a whelk. He grunted and jerked back, staring in disbelief. She reached for him, but he pushed her hand away and got up, angrily pulling up his pants and zipping his fly. As he made for the door she – stupidly, she realised – said, "Jas? What about your tea?" at which he picked up the plate and flung it hard at the wall. The baby began to cry. Jason slammed the front door. Sharon took a deep breath, put on her skirt, and picked up the sausage and broken china and most of the chips. She put them in the kitchen bin, then got a cloth and dabbed half-heartedly at the baked beans oozing down the wall.

*

Jason headed for the pub, pushing out of his mind the fact that what had seemed to put him off at the last minute was Sharon's body – the fact that it was female.

It was early, the bar almost empty. He ordered a pint. The barman was new, clean-shaven, neatly dressed and good-looking. Poofter, thought Jason. He drank half the beer and sat moodily watching the barman serving in the saloon. He only looked about nineteen, tall, slim, with a small, neat arse. Jason started to feel randy again. He made himself think about Sharon, although he was watching the barman's bum. He thought about Sharon's bum. He finished his beer, and went back home.

She was sitting on the bed reading a magazine, still naked under her skirt. He threw the magazine aside, pulling up her skirt as he unzipped. He shut his eyes as he thrust, and this time almost made it, but not quite. Her femaleness was too insistent. She began to sympathise, which was the last straw. He smacked her across the face, and stumbled out, pulling up his trousers; he went to the off-licence for a bottle of Scotch, took it home, and drank himself insensible in the living room.

*

Two days after that, on the bus to work, Jason suddenly caught his breath, and jerked his thighs together. It felt as if – something – were in his underpants. He looked down, not knowing what he expected to see, but all he saw was the crotch of his trousers slightly stirred by the beginnings of arousal. He felt a hand – a small, smooth hand – stroking his balls, fondling his prick, expertly turning him on. The pleasure, though, was utterly drowned in embarrassment, bewilderment and horror. He had to stand and walk very awkwardly getting off the bus, and breathed a huge sigh of relief as the hand ceased its attentions as he entered the workshop, and his excitement diminished before any of his workmates could notice. He tried to put the experience out of his mind, telling himself he'd been drinking too much, that his failure to get it up with Sharon was affecting his mind. Perhaps he should find a tart – but to be embarrassed like that with a tart would be worse, and cost money as well. It was just one of those things. He wouldn't think about it.

But the hand came back, next day, and the days after, at work, on the bus. Jason began to acquire a permanently hunched posture, and inevitably had to endure crude cracks from the blokes at work. He stayed away from the pub for a few days, but he found it wasn't only the barman; everywhere, he was conscious of young men in tight jeans, the slight bulge at the crotch, the way their buttocks moved against each other. The hard-on seldom lasted till he got back to Sharon; once when it did, he told her to take off her skirt and tights and put her jeans on. She stared at him.

"Are you stupid?" he shouted, "I want to fuck you in your jeans. Is that too hard to understand? Can you hear me?"

She went on staring, but backed away and went into the bedroom. He followed her and as she got the jeans halfway up, he pushed her face first against the wall with one hand, freeing himself with the other, and entered her from behind, his eyes closed, in his mind thrusting between the cheeks of a plump, pretty boy. He came, cataclysmically, and immediately went to the bathroom and was sick.

He didn't try again. He masturbated a lot, and took out his feeling of helplessness in smacking Sharon and shaking the baby when it cried. One morning when he was too hungover to protest, Sharon said, why didn't he go to the doctor?

"Yeah," Jason said, "that's likely." What would he say? Doctor, I can't get it up with a woman? Doctor I'm suddenly turning queer? Yeah, right.

He tried to keep telling himself it was Sharon that was the problem, and wondered if he should try and pick up one of the slags they met down the pub, but he knew he wouldn't. The humiliation would be public then.

After another couple of weeks, Jason came home and found the flat empty. He cursed, wondering who Sharon was out gossiping with. Her bloody sister or her mum, or that bitch Kayley. There was no food in the kitchen; he cursed again and went out for a kebab. It wasn't till he was eating it in front of the TV that he noticed an *emptiness* on the shelf unit next to the set, where Sharon's Mills and Boons and fat chick-lit paperbacks lived. He puzzled about it till he finished his meal then went into the bedroom. A lot of clothes were gone from the wardrobe; the baby's things were gone; in the bathroom, the shelves were practically empty.

When he realised she wasn't coming back it was almost a relief. He made no attempt to find her. He lived on takeaways and slept a lot.

*

There was a new apprentice at work, just sixteen, with soft yellow hair and a pink and white prettiness. Jason couldn't help seeing him, all the time. The desire grew – and the hand got to work, stroking and fondling. He went to the toilet and tried to masturbate himself to orgasm, but his excitement abated as soon as he was on his own. He went back and the hand began again. Just before lunchtime it brought him to a climax.

He felt himself blushing scarlet. The men were sniggering, and when he looked up he found the supervisor giving him a filthy look. At lunch break he muttered to the supervisor that he had food poisoning and left without waiting for an answer. He went to the library and found Lenny, reading the papers. He'd finished the *Sun* and started on the *Mirror*.

Jason said, "Come down the pub."

"What, now?" said Lenny, in a library whisper.

"They're open all day, aren't they? Come on."

It was three pints and a whisky chaser before he could start to talk about it. "Len," he said, "what'd you say if I told you I was … I was … haunted?"

Lenny started and slopped his beer. "Haunted? What d'you mean? What by?"

"Well ... by … by a hand, I suppose."

"Oh God. Oh God. It's got you too, then."

Hesitantly, they told each other the things the hand had done, the terrible appetites it had aroused. After a couple more drinks Jason went to the gents. Lenny followed him in.

When they had finished urinating they looked at each other. The toilet was empty. Without a word they went into a cubicle and bolted the door. Gently, lovingly, unwillingly, in the cramped and stinking stall, they touched each other, kissed, undressed, handled and sucked and pleasured each other...

Afterwards, white-faced, silent, they walked out of the pub in opposite directions.

*

Jason went back to his empty flat and hanged himself with his belt. Sharon found him a week later when she returned for the rest of her shoes.

Lenny, who was too stupid to be a pessimist, went

home to his mum and knocked her down out of habit, and locked himself in his bedroom. Over the next few days his behaviour was so bizarre that when his mum called the police, after he threw a saucepan of boiling cabbage at her and knocked himself unconscious trying to fling himself out of a closed window, she persuaded them to section him. She put it all down to drugs.

In the hospital he lay still, masturbating constantly, and never speaking except when he looked up, smiled sweetly, and said, "Hallo, Grandad."

Forward and Back, Change Places

Paul walked from the tube station through the north London dusk, climbed the stone steps, and looked around as he entered the hall. He hadn't been here for years, not since he'd moved south of the river, but tonight a particularly good ceilidh band was playing and he felt the urge to dance. The band was setting up; already quite a few people were sitting about the room and chatting. Paul saw a few vaguely familiar faces, but no-one he knew well enough to go and talk to. He put his coat down on a seat and went to get a beer.

He sat out the first two dances but then got up his nerve to ask a middle-aged woman he recognised from somewhere. After that he found it easier, and since there was as usual a shortage of men he found a partner for every dance before the interval.

The bar was packed in the break so Paul went into the side room where they served tea and cake and sandwiches. This was emptier but there were no free tables, so he took his tea and fruitcake to a corner table where a plump, dark man was sitting alone. "Excuse me, do you mind if I sit here?"

"Go ahead!" The dark man beamed. Paul wondered if he were looking for someone to talk to, and hoped he wasn't a bore. Paul wasn't good at getting away from bores. He sat down, stirred his tea, although he didn't take sugar, and broke a piece off his cake.

The dark man said, "Haven't seen you here before, have I?"

"No, I don't get up here often."

"Come far?"

"Not so far. Takes me an hour or so." Warily not saying where he lived, until he knew whether the other were a bore or not.

"Ah! I live quite close. Good band, aren't they?"

"Very good. Came to hear them, really. Very good to dance to."

"I'm Gilbert."

He held out his hand and Paul felt obliged to take it, saying, "Paul."

However, the subsequent conversation was quite pleasant and Gilbert did not reveal any particular obsession or monotony of thought. Paul finished his tea and cake and stood up.

Gilbert said, "Enjoy the second half," as though he were not staying, and Paul went back into the hall.

She must have come in during the interval. She was already whirling round in a Cumberland Square Eight when he saw her – tall, slim, with long, red hair. He only caught a glimpse of her face, but it did something to him. He sat down, feeling a little dizzy; he hadn't felt like that about anyone since he was fourteen, and tried to pull himself together. The dance finished; she walked off with a group of people and while he was still wondering if he dared go and ask her to dance, she stood up again with a tall fair-haired man in a blue shirt. Paul was still staring at that end of the room when a voice said, "Are you doing this one?" He turned and saw one of the women he'd danced with earlier. He stood up – he wasn't sure what they danced, but it was one he knew and he didn't make any major mistakes.

By the time it finished, he'd decided he must get a grip. He would try to speak to the red-haired woman; it would be ridiculous not to dance as much as possible now he'd come all this way. No doubt once he spoke to her she would turn out to be quite ordinary. He determined to enjoy the rest of the evening, and succeeded pretty well; he glimpsed her often, but she was always in another set. He thought he might catch her up in a circle dance where the women changed partners, but she was still two couples away when the music stopped. At the end of the evening they were in the same set for Drops of Brandy, and he thought he *must* get to swing her by the arm at least once – but some other couple went wrong, and suddenly she was moving away from him again.

At the end, someone spoke to him and when he looked round again she was nowhere to be seen. Oh well, he sighed, that was that. He put on his coat and made for the bus stop, expecting to forget the whole thing.

*

He didn't forget, though. The thought of the woman with red hair kept coming back, and the magical feeling he'd had at the sight of her. No matter how he told himself she would be quite ordinary if he spoke to her, she stayed in his mind until there was nothing for him to do but return to the next month's ceilidh and hope that she might be there. If he did that, he would have done all he could; but he must do that.

*

He was rather later this time; the dancing had already started, and he saw her on the far side of the hall, partnering the tall fair man again. If she had a boyfriend there was really no point in speaking to her at all. Paul found a seat and took off his coat. At the end of that dance he tried to work up the courage simply to walk across the room and stand near her, and perhaps start a conversation with someone in the same group, but his heart was pounding ridiculously and by the time he was halfway there they were making up sets for the next dance.

It went on like that through the first half; between dances he would work his way towards her, and then she would move off suddenly, or he would get in a conversation and not know how to end it. Somehow he was again never in the same set, except once, in a longways dance, where he followed her at five couples distance from one end to the other. The dance ended before she and her partner turned and came back. It was maddening, and the more it happened the worse his nerves became. At the interval, he thought he might manage to find her in the bar, but she wasn't there. He looked into the tea room: she was sitting at the far side, at a table with four other people, all talking animatedly. Paul sighed, bought a cup of tea, and saw Gilbert, once more sitting on his own. Gilbert greeted Paul cheerfully, and they chatted about the band, and the weather. Gilbert said, "Wasn't expecting to see you here again."

"Oh well, it was good last time and there's not much in the way of dancing near me. It's only about half an hour on the tube, nothing really." That was only half the journey but he didn't want it to sound as if he'd made an enormous effort.

"Ah," said Gilbert, "that's good. Maybe you'll get into the habit."

Paul smiled. "Maybe I shall."

"You're on your own, are you?"

"What? Yes, I came on my own."

"No, I mean, you live on your own? You're not married?"

"Er, no." Paul was bit taken aback. He's not making a pass, is he? Or looking for a flat share?

"Sorry, perhaps that sounded a bit rude. I'm just interested. Interested in people, you know."

"Oh, right. No, I'm not married. Plenty of time for that."

"Oh, of course."

Was it his imagination, or did Gilbert look at him a bit oddly? No – imagination, must be.

"Divorced, me. Didn't work out. Mind you, I'd marry again. Not easy to find the right woman."

"No, no, it's not, is it?" Paul really didn't want to talk about women or his love life, or lack thereof. He finished his tea, and murmured something about going to the gents.

He saw Gilbert a couple of times in the second half, not dancing but sitting and watching the dancers, a bit sadly, perhaps, but Paul really didn't feel he was under any obligation to go and sit with him. He had plenty of partners – he was a good dancer, though he would blush to say so – and the enjoyment of dancing took over even from the anxious watching for the red-haired woman. His heart sank absurdly, though, when he finished a final polka with a girl from Ealing and realised that the red-haired woman, the fair man, and the rest of the people they'd been with had all gone.

He wandered over to fetch his coat, feeling near to tears. Ridiculous, he said to himself, when he'd never even seen the woman up close, and she appeared to be spoken for anyway. She was a good dancer, true; but the room was full of tolerably good dancers. He put his coat on, and walked with dragging footsteps to the door. As he left, he realised Gilbert was beside him.

"You OK? You look a bit sick."

"I'm fine. Just tired. Miserable weather for June, isn't it?"

"Oh well. Not so bad. Paul, I know this is none of my business, but I couldn't help noticing. At tea time, you kept looking at the table in the corner. Is there ... I mean, have you got a problem with somebody?"

"What? Oh – no, not really. I just ... there was someone I thought I knew, that's all."

"Ah?"

Having given himself this lead in, he thought he might continue – there was always a chance Gilbert might know who she was. "The girl with the long red hair. I've got a feeling I've seen her somewhere before, but I can't think where. You don't know her, I suppose?"

"Long red hair –? Um, no, I'm afraid not, no. Well. See you next month?"

"Yes, maybe."

Gilbert turned aside at a bus stop and Paul continued to the tube station, his mind in a pitiable state.

*

The next month seemed to drag on for years. Work was unexciting and Paul could find very little to do in his spare time. He watched a lot of television. He wondered if it were worth going to the hall to the other events, in case she went to something else there. But what? He went to a dance one Thursday but she wasn't there. Being in the same building without her presence just made the misery worse. It was all so pointless, he told himself; but that didn't make any difference.

Sometimes he had a positive day, when he assured himself that next month she would be there, and he would speak to her – somehow he would make the opportunity, and he wouldn't dance with anyone until he'd done it. If he made sure of where she was sitting and stationed himself nearby, sooner or later, surely, there would be a chance to smile and say, "Hallo. I've seen you here before," or something, *something*, however naff...

But other times he was sure she wouldn't be there

again, or if he spoke to her she would stare at him and turn away... He was, let's face it, short and slight and nondescript, he thought. He rather imagined people thought of him as "that dreadful weedy little man", though he had no evidence that they did.

Then something a colleague said at work gave him another dreadful thought: would she think he was stalking her if he hung about until he had a chance to speak? Was he, in fact, a stalker? Was that what it meant – this obsession with someone you didn't know? Obsession, infatuation – it was only love at first sight if you both felt it... Oh God. Perhaps he'd better not go to the next ceilidh at all....

When the time came, though, he couldn't face the thought of not going. He would go, he would speak to her, and then he would leave – or at least go to the bar, and keep out of her way.

He arrived early, in fact far too early and had to go and sit in the bar as nothing else was open. As he glumly started a pint of beer someone sat down opposite him, and he looked up to see Gilbert's round, pink, amiable face.

"Hallo Paul. You're early."

"Mm, yes, I allowed far too much time for the journey. Thought it would be busy, the weather's so fine. Very hot on the tube."

"Must be."

Gilbert seemed distracted. Paul said, "So how are you? Everything OK?"

"Oh yes. Well..." Gilbert fiddled with a beer mat before saying, "Paul. Do you believe in ghosts?"

"What? No, I don't think so. Why?"

"It can be a problem, you know. People who come back, and ... who aren't there."

"I suppose it could be. But I can't say I believe in it, you know."

"No. No, I suppose not. I shan't trouble you, then. Excuse me, I have to go and speak to someone…" He wandered off and Paul sat frowning into his beer. Odd subject to bring up. Oh well, when he'd finished this pint the hall should be open.

She wasn't there at the start and Paul had a bad half hour thinking she wasn't coming; but at the end of a set of Nottingham Swing he saw a flurry of people in the doorway, and among them an unmistakable figure and a glow of red hair. As Paul chatted to his erstwhile partner, he watched out of the corner of his eye and marked where she put her handbag down. When the next dance started he went to the gents and when he returned he walked – he hoped unobtrusively – round the room and sat down a yard or two from her bag. She didn't sit down between that dance and the next, but at the end of the second she walked straight past him, looked at him, and smiled. He smiled back but was quite unable to speak. She picked up her handbag and left the hall.

She hadn't returned by the interval and Paul thought of simply sitting there, stubbornly, waiting for her, but then Gilbert came by and said, "Cup of tea?" and Paul couldn't think of an excuse not to go.

He hunched miserably over his tea, and Gilbert said cautiously, "Paul? There is something wrong, isn't there?"

"Well, yes. But it's silly."

"I won't laugh."

"It's just that I'm … infatuated with this woman. I don't even know her, I haven't spoken to her. It's silly. I'll get over it. It's just … it's nothing."

"Ah. I see. Is it, by any chance, the red-haired woman you mentioned last time?"

"Yes. Yes, it is. She is very attractive, isn't she? But she seems to have a boyfriend, so there's not much I can do anyway."

"Ah, no. No, I imagine not. Look, Paul, now don't take this the wrong way, but I ... I haven't actually seen this woman you're talking about."

"Oh! I'm sorry. I thought you said you saw her last month – when I asked if you knew who she was."

"Well, no. That's the thing —"

Paul had turned and looked round the room. "Look," he said, "she's just over there by the door, talking to that woman with the white hair and the peasant blouse —" He turned back and saw Gilbert not looking towards the door, but gazing rather worriedly at Paul.

"What?"

"Paul. There's no-one there."

"What are you talking about?"

"There is a woman with white hair, just going out of the door. She's on her own."

"Don't be ridiculous —" He turned again, and there was no-one in the doorway. "She's gone back to the hall. She was there a minute ago."

"Paul. You have to believe me. Look, there are ... people who ... who aren't really there, but who make you believe they are ... they do it to mess with your head. You must believe me, Paul; really, you must."

"What? What do you mean, not really there? What are you talking about?"

"Sometimes they're people who ... who were alive and when they're ... not, they can't leave. They can't go from the place where they were alive."

Paul was staring at him. "You're telling me she's a *ghost*?"

"For want of a better word."

"You're mad. No, sorry, but look, I've seen her

dancing. I mean, the people she's dancing with must be able to see her – they'd notice, you know? She can't just be visible to me."

"Maybe, maybe not. I can't say. But look, just think about the possibility. I mean, listen, the way she's ... she's enthralled you. Is that natural? Has that ever happened before?"

"Not as such, no. But..." It was crazy. She'd walked by him. He'd felt the air move as she passed by. Hadn't he? On the other hand, she was somehow always on the other side of the room... Oh no, absurd. "Look, are you sure? I mean, maybe you've just missed seeing her."

"Really. I know about these things. You should be careful. As I said, they mess with you head. They like to upset you. Cause you grief. You must be careful." Gilbert was gazing at him, obviously desperately concerned.

Paul shook his head, sat back. "I don't know," he said, "I really don't know. I honestly can't believe what you're saying, but... Let me think about it."

"Of course. But just do me a favour: don't make any more attempts to speak to her, to get closer to her. It could be very dangerous."

"Dangerous?"

"You see, sometimes the reason these people stay around is because they like to play with people. Manipulate them. They can't leave anything alone. If you get close to them, get involved, let them influence you – it won't end happily, I promise."

Paul shook his head again. "I don't know. I... OK, OK, I'll keep away from her for the time being," thinking, Fat chance of anything else. Suddenly he couldn't bear Gilbert looking concernedly at him any longer; he got up, and moved towards the hall. The red-haired girl and the fair man were leaving. He stared as they went through the door and realised they were putting up umbrellas; it had started to rain. Surely ghosts didn't need umbrellas? Gilbert was still looking at Paul, still worried.

Paul took a deep breath, said nothing, and went into the hall for his waterproof.

Gilbert waited at the outer door; they walked in silence to the bus stop. As they parted, Gilbert said, "Just think of what I've said. Be careful."

"I will. But I honestly can't... Never mind. See you next month."

"It's closed in August."

"Whatever." He realised he was being rude but he couldn't stand another word; he plunged off through the rain to the tube station.

*

August was hot and wet and unbearable. She was in his mind more than ever. He was supposed to go to a folk festival but he stayed home watching television, remembering her face as she smiled at him. Perhaps, he thought, Gilbert's warning was too late – he was caught, he would waste away, like the lovers of La Belle Dame Sans Merci. Perhaps he would join her, haunting the place for the rest of time. Life had become something to be struggled through – but death might be no improvement.

He must go back in September and ask Gilbert if he knew any way of getting free of her enchantment. Maybe he could get exorcised, or something... Round and round in his head, the thought of her, and then the fear of what she might be, and then the thought of her again, till he didn't know which way was up.

*

September was fine and warm, but he hesitated about going and arrived well after the start. He took off his coat and deliberately didn't look round. A longways set had just finished and he was about to make for the nearest empty seat when a voice said, "Paul! Man alive, what brings you here from darkest Plumstead?"

He turned, and saw a stocky woman with short dark hair – Alice, whom he'd known at college. He was delighted to see someone he was sure was real, and beamed at her.

"Hi. Haven't seen you in a parrot's lifetime. Are you still in London?"

"I'm back – been working in Manchester for six months. Didn't think you came here?"

"Only started recently. There's not much down my way."

"Well, good to see you. Oh – this is Steve, and his sister Sam."

And suddenly he was being introduced to the tall fair man and the red-haired woman. He felt dizzy, and hoped he managed to make sense. He shook Sam's hand. It felt real. Alice, surely, hadn't become a ghost – he'd have heard something. Sam had a distinct Wolverhampton accent which to his besotted mind was wholly beautiful.

Alice was saying, "Sam's just down from the Midlands, which are sodden and unkind, working at my place. We've known each other over the phone for a couple of years. Come on Steve, I like this one."

And she hauled him off, leaving Paul to dance with Sam; and it went on like that till the interval, when they all went for a cup of tea – Sam didn't drink alcohol. Paul looked round the tearoom for Gilbert, but couldn't see him. The table in the corner was empty.

Steve got a tray of teas and cakes and biscuits and they sat down at a large table, but Paul couldn't help looking over his shoulder.

Sam said, "You usually sit over there, don't you?"

Good lord, she'd noticed him. "Er, yes. I suppose I do."

"I saw you a couple of times, and I nearly came over, you were so on your own, but you didn't really look as if you wanted company?"

"What?"

"Sorry, I don't mean to be rude, but you were always sitting on your own when I saw you."

"What? Oh … you didn't see anyone with me? A shortish bloke with brown hair?"

She frowned. "No."

"Oh..." A horrible thought started to grow in his mind. On your own. People who aren't there. They mess with your head. His stomach turned and his vision darkened; he felt like a man who thinks he is walking on a broad, safe path, till the sun rises and he sees the sheer drop inches from his feet. They mess with your head...

"Are you all right? You've gone white." Sam's voice recalled him and he shuddered. She took his hand and hers was warm and slightly rough, with a callous on the index finger. He stared at it, and took a few deep breaths.

"I'm fine. Yeah. I'm fine. Just a bit dizzy for a minute"

"You sure?"

"Sure. It's a bit hot in here, and I didn't get round to eating before I came out."

"D'you want a sandwich or something?"

He looked at her, the concern in her clear brown eyes, took another deep breath, and turned for a moment at the sudden feeling that someone was standing behind him, that Gilbert would come up and touch him on the shoulder... There was no-one behind him. Gilbert was nowhere in the room. Paul turned back and shook his head.

"I'm fine. I'll have another bit of cake. And believe me, I do like company. But some people's more than others."

He smiled, hesitantly. She smiled back, accepting the compliment; and his own smile grew wider and assured.

District to Upminster

Sami had a theory, which he started explaining as we passed the barrier at Richmond.

"Speed," he said, "speed beyond a certain point isn't natural. It upsets the waves of reality."

"Upsets the what?"

"Reality is a construct. The intersection of time, space, magnetic fields and mental projection."

"What does that mean?"

He looked at me and sighed. "If I explained," he said, "would you understand?"

"Probably not."

The pigeon got on just before we started, and it pottered about, pecking rather inefficiently at discarded chips and kebabs on the unswept floor. I watched it for a bit, while Sami went on explaining his theory, despite his conviction that I wouldn't understand it.

"GK Chesterton," he said suddenly – well he probably didn't, it just swam suddenly up out of the stream of what he was saying, as something I'd heard before. "GK Chesterton, you told me once he wrote that it was a miracle that a train to Victoria actually went to Victoria."

"Yeah. I think he might have been exaggerating a bit – I mean in principle he regarded it as a miracle, but he probably wasn't that astonished when he got there." Or maybe he was just astonished to find he'd got on the right train. However.

"He was right," said Sami. "Every time a train gets where it's going, it's a victory for the human will over the forces of randomness."

"I suppose it is." I wasn't really thinking much about it, as I was distracted by looking out of the window, and thinking the station we were just leaving should have been Turnham Green and didn't look like it. I checked the map; maybe Turnham Green was closed. The map had been taken down. It was getting dark, so I couldn't see a lot outside once we'd left the station.

"We've passed the point at which the technology is controllable by human strength, you see."

"Have we? What point was that?" I was distracted again by two men behind me talking very loudly about the Test match.

"Some time in the twentieth century —"

Sami was drowned out by a large party of men in white robes, arguing loudly as they walked down the carriage. The lights dimmed as they got to the end, and I didn't see what happened to them. I was beginning to wonder if I'd had too much gin. The pigeon looked up at me, only it was a pied crow, and I was sure that hadn't been there before.

I looked out of the window again. A long level grassland stretched away from the track, and in the middle distance a large group of horsemen were galloping, keeping pace with the train. It didn't, somehow, look like Ravenscourt Park. At the end of the carriage two men were sitting, handcuffed together.

I said to Sami, "Where are we?"

"What?"

"Where are we? I mean what's the next station?"

He glanced at the window and said, "West Kensington. Look, are you listening?"

"Oh yes. But like you said, I don't really follow all of it. As far as I can understand it you're saying that the technology is now out of our control, and it could be doing anything. This train is no more likely to finish up at Upminster than at Ongar or Manchester Piccadilly or Gdansk."

He sighed. "I knew you'd oversimplify. You just don't do abstract, do you? It's always got to be a concrete example."

"That's the way I think. You know that."

The pied crow was now an ibis, and the window was obscured by people clinging to the outside of the train. It looked very hot out there, somehow. We went into a tunnel and all the lights went out. I thought very hard about Earl's Court. Sami went on talking. I closed my eyes and concentrated.

When I opened them we were pulling into a station; it was almost Earl's Court but not quite. A couple who looked just like Trevor Howard and Celia Johnson were standing beside the train, gazing into each other's eyes. I wasn't terribly surprised. The pigeon was back, though, looking a bit confused. I looked out again as we started; some of it seemed right. I saw the sign that says Tower Hill – Stops Here – Barking; and then I remembered they'd changed the indicators and it shouldn't have looked like that.

Gloucester Road seemed to be full of refugees, but that might have been an art installation. I didn't manage to notice South Ken because a fight broke out and a passing waiter dropped a tray of drinks on Sami's briefcase. He got angry about it without apparently noticing that drinks waiters on District Line trains were an unusual sight, to say the least. I wondered fleetingly if he carried the abstract thing too far. The carriage was very full and there was a lot of jostling. Sloane Square is always dark, anyway – could have been anywhere. I pinned my hopes to Victoria. I concentrated very hard, thinking about GK

Chesterton, and the human will, and I probably prayed a bit too. I tried to picture Victoria Station, as it were, in essence, without too many details that I might get wrong. I concentrated on the pigeon being a pigeon, too. I found I had to keep pushing a picture of Isambard Kingdom Brunel out of my head.

My concentration was broken by Sami's elbow in my ribs. "Come on, this is Victoria, we get out here."

It looked all right, so far as I could tell. We were supposed to change and get the Victoria Line, but I said I'd got claustrophobia and insisted on getting a bus. I was feeling tired, and I wasn't sure I could keep us going to Oxford Circus.

I was a bit worried about the man in the stovepipe hat I saw at the top of the escalator.

The Cupboard of Winds

The first thing I noticed was when the radio cleared its throat. I don't sleep well and tend to leave the radio on all night, so when I wake up at five in the morning it's there. I was just wishing I could sleep for another couple of hours, when in one of those pauses between discs, I heard this throat-clearing. First I thought, That's odd; then I thought, The presenter must have left the mic on, or not realised the piece has finished. Then a voice said, "Are you awake?"

I realised then that I must be still asleep and dreaming so I said, "No." And saying it woke me up.

The radio said, "Good. It's about the draughts."

"What?"

"You must have noticed how draughty this house is. Haven't you wondered where it's coming from?"

"Uh." I'm talking to the radio. It's talking to me. I *must* be dreaming. OK, it's one of those dreams where you think you've woken up but you haven't. "Yeah. Yeah, it's a very draughty house. I've tried putting stuff round the doors. It doesn't seem to come from the windows. Maybe it's air currents. From the radiators. Um, who are you?"

"Who I am doesn't matter." I'm listening to the voice now; it's male, cultured, hard to tell the age. "Just find out."

Then the music cut back in. I decided to get up, make a cup of tea and go back to sleep, so that when I woke up I'd know I was awake.

It is a draughty house. It doesn't worry me most of the time; I prefer older buildings. This one is about 1890, terrace house, well built, original windows; you accept they're not going to be airtight, and it means I don't worry so much about carbon monoxide poisoning from the boiler. But the conversation in the dream stayed in my mind and I started taking more notice of all the random little cold air currents around the place. I had vaguely assumed that they were coming down the chimneys, and escaping through imperfectly blocked off fireplaces or, as I'd said in the dream, air movement created by the radiators. But I started noticing how they would spring up when it was quite still outside, and the direction – well, more often than not they came from the upstairs landing. Hot air rises, I thought, so I suppose cold air sinks. I didn't entirely convince myself, though.

That was when Danny and I had the conversation about living together. I wasn't, to be honest, entirely sure I wanted to; but when Danny said it wasn't going to happen in this house because of the draughts – his exact words were, "If you think I'm moving into this fecking icebox with the Arctic gales you must be joking" – I got riled. I suppose we both said things that were not very polite. It wasn't quite, "If you loved me you wouldn't care about the draughts", but anyway, it put an end to the relationship. Which in the long term was probably a good thing, but the long term is the long term.

Whatever, it made me more pissed off about the draughts; and not long after that, when I'd spent an evening drowning my sorrows a bit, I decided I would track down the draught once and for all. It had to be coming from somewhere. I lit a scented candle and with that in one hand and a half-full bottle of vodka in the other I went upstairs; the draught was definitely coming down the stairs.

When I got to the landing I waved the candle about –

none too steadily, I suspect, and none too safely either. The draught was plainly blowing from one side of the landing; it was blowing, in fact, from a large cupboard. You'd think it's an airing cupboard, being where it is, but it's not, and it's too shallow from front to back to be a lot of use for anything. It tended to fill up with stuff I couldn't be arsed to throw out, or that I use once or twice a year: Christmas decorations, board games, old greeting cards, the remains of a coffee set of my great-aunt's, a broken tennis racket, magazines I'm going to throw out when I'm sure I don't need to keep them – you know the sort of thing.

Now here's the problem. This cupboard is on an inside wall, and it doesn't have a chimney. So there couldn't be a draught blowing out of it, right? I put down the candle, which promptly blew out, and opened the cupboard door.

Inside was quite a large space, dusty and untidy, and still containing the things that should have been in there, but considerably larger than when I last looked. In the middle, sitting on a heap of old magazines, was a tall, pale woman.

I was so gobsmacked I didn't even have the brain function to scream.

She looked up, rather startled, and said, "You can see me," then she spotted the vodka bottle and said, "Ah, you have brought a libation!"

I handed her the bottle. It seemed the obvious thing to do. I was a bit shocked when she drained it in one swallow, gave a deep sigh, handed me back the empty bottle and said, "That's better. I haven't had a libation in centuries. Have you come to worship me?"

"Umm, no, I don't think so." My head was still trying to get round the huge space where my cupboard used to be. "Who are you?"

"Who am I? Good Hera, you've brought me a libation and you don't know who I am?"

"Well. It seemed the – the right thing." What am I talking about? I thought.

"You're right, of course. I am Aura, Goddess of the Breeze."

"Oh!" I said before I could stop myself. "You're the draught."

"Or," she said, with narrower eyes, "Goddess of Draughts. Yes."

"What are you doing in my cupboard?"

"*Your* cupboard? My dear woman, this cupboard's been here a great deal longer than you have."

"Oh yes." Well I could hardly deny it. "Have you lived in it all the time it's been here, then?"

"A good deal longer than that. If you humans choose to build houses on ancient sacred sites you have to expect to make allowances. We've still got to live somewhere. A lot of the pantheon took themselves off, but I thought, No, why should I? Britain's a remarkably breezy place – draughty if you prefer – so I feel at home here. Have you any more libation?"

"I think there's some gin downstairs. Why don't you live in the drinks cupboard?" Again the words were out before I could stop them.

She shrugged. "It's too cramped. And until now I've had a bit of privacy in this one."

I went down to get the gin.

While I was going, I thought – or the vodka thought – that I must – *must* – ask her to leave. It was intolerable. She had no right to be in my cupboard, even if she had been there for hundreds of years. She had no tenancy agreement. She could drink the gin and go. I'm not sure I was being very logical, you understand, but it seemed to make sense at the time.

When I came back, Aura was still there; a part of my mind said she wouldn't. She was reading an old copy of *Marie Claire*.

She looked up. "You realise I've read this three times? Why do you never put anything new in here?"

"Sorry." I poured the gin into two glasses and said, "Do you mind if I join you?"

She looked surprised but said, "No – no, if you wish. Do you want a blessing or a boon? Because I don't do much of that any more."

"Well..." It was kind of awkward, I realised. I was sobering up a bit and the fact that I was sitting drinking gin with a personified draught was doing my head in, but it was still awkward. Asking a lodger who doesn't pay the rent to move out is difficult enough for me. "Well," I said again, "I don't suppose you'd consider finding alternative accommodation?"

"What?" She frowned. "Oh! You want me to *leave*?"

"It's just that the house is awfully draughty."

"I must say you've got a nerve. I've been here for over a thousand years and you're asking me to move because it's draughty."

"If you put it like that..."

"You do realise, don't you, that I keep the imps away?" She looked at me rather sternly.

"Pardon?"

"The – what do you call them now? Gremlins? Brownies? The small creatures that move things. Haven't you noticed while you've lived here that things are always where you left them?"

In fact, I had noticed but I'd thought in my ignorance that I must be getting a bit more organised. "Oh," I said, "that's you, is it?"

"The lesser creatures keep away from the neighbourhood of deity. I may be a minor goddess but they still avoid me."

"Right. Well, that – that's good. Yes." I considered whether that was worth the draught. Then I thought of something else. "Someone ... the other day..."

"Yes?"

"A voice. From the radio. It told me to find out where the draught was coming from."

Aura stiffened, the glass of gin in her hand, and said in a remote voice, "Leave me."

"What?"

"Leave me. The rage of gods is not for mortals to witness."

I stood up and made to shut the cupboard door. Before I did so I remembered to put the bottle of gin inside.

*

Fortunately there was some cherry vodka in the kitchen that I'd forgotten about. I had a couple of glasses to steady my nerves. I finally steadied them enough to pass out for a few hours, even without the radio. In the morning ... all right ... afternoon (fortunately it was Saturday) I woke up rather carefully, with a definite sense of looming menace. At first I thought it was just the sense of looming menace with which I always wake up, then I remembered, there's a goddess of draughts in the landing cupboard. I felt my way carefully downstairs – I wasn't able to open my eyes fully yet – and made some tea.

After several mugs of tea and a bowl of cereal I was sort of awake, but I couldn't exactly say I was coping. I kept saying to myself as I washed and dressed – aloud, in the hope it would sound more plausible, "There's a Goddess of Draughts in the landing cupboard and I've asked her to leave. On the one hand she keeps the wossnames away and I can find things, on the other hand it's bloody draughty and it's ruining my love life. And she's drunk all the gin."

Eventually the moment arrived where I had either to panic and leave the house, possibly never to return, or to confront the cupboard. I took a bottle of cooking sherry, collected some magazines, and went upstairs.

She was still there. She looked up from a copy of *New Scientist* that I'd put in there the week before and said, "It's that bloody Aeolus, isn't it? Not satisfied with bundling us all up in a bag and giving us to that idiot Odysseus, he's been chasing us round ever since, trying to get us back under control. He's the God of Air, you see – that's how he's able to take over the radio. Airwaves. He wants you to drive me out, then he can chase me back to that bloody cave. I mean, it's not the bloody Hilton in here, but it's better than a bloody cave." She unscrewed the bottle top and took a mouthful of sherry. "The libations are a damn sight better too."

I noticed, without paying attention, that while we were talking, the draughts dropped a bit; but when she started to get angry about Aeolus, half a gale blew out of the cupboard.

"I brought some more to read," I said hastily, handing in a bag of miscellaneous copies of the *Radio Times*, free newspapers and *Big Issue*s. She looked somewhat disparaging.

"They'll do for the time being," she said. "I realise no-one's going to come and recite to a lute in here..."

I asked her, "Why is Aeolus talking to me? I mean, if he can't persuade you to go back to the cave, what can I do? By the way, I mislaid a new toothbrush this morning."

"He has no shame. If he hasn't persuaded the imps back in, he probably stole it himself. Maybe he's promised them theocratic immunity. He can't force me out, you know. But if I leave, well, where would I go? It's not so easy to find somewhere to be inconspicuous in London these days. Property prices are so high, everyone's making use of every inch of space. Finding another cupboard no-one opens from one week's end to the next is almost impossible. Ten to one I'd end up in the bloody cave."

"I see," I said, the way you do when you have no clue.

She poured some cooking sherry into the gin glass. "Well?" she said, "Are you going to let me stay? You can't let that autocratic son of a demi-god drag me back – can you?"

"Er ... I – ah, the phone's ringing, I'd better answer it." I fled downstairs, feeling cornered. I hate being appealed to.

The phone call was from Danny. "Hi sweet," he said, "how's the icebox?" Diplomatic, is Danny.

"Fine," I said. "I've been talking to the draught."

"Sorry?"

"Never mind. How are you doing?"

"Oh fine, things are great. Just thought I'd see how you were, wondered if you were doing anything tonight?"

"Um, nothing really."

"Fancy going to the pictures? I ... I thought you might like to see the new *Star Trek* movie. If you haven't seen it."

"No, I haven't. Yeah, that'd be good." I did want to see it; and I also wanted to know what Danny's motive was in asking me; so we arranged to meet at the cinema.

I went back upstairs but the cupboard door was shut and I left it that way.

Danny's motive turned out to be nothing unexpected; he was feeling lonely, and missing regular sex, and his default setting was still to ring me up. He wasn't any more inclined to move in, although he was willing to brave the draughts for a bit of nookie. On the way home I realised that he was still hunky and probably still good in bed, but that I couldn't be bothered. I started to say goodnight and he got pathetic on me and tried to pretend he really missed me, and all that, and I got irritated. I said, "Look, if you want to come in for a shag, say so. Don't make out it's going to be romantic when it isn't, all right?" I like to know where I am with things.

Instead of telling the truth, he chose to take offence and stomped off. I was mostly glad but between sexual tension and anger I was too wound up to sleep, so I put the radio on. I was just starting to relax when Aeolus' voice interrupted the Rachmaninov. "Well, you see how things are now. Do you want it to go on?"

"What? Oh, yes." I was irritated again now. "Why is this so important to you? I mean, it's been a ridiculously long time, why can't you just let it go?"

"Time is nothing to the gods. Let it go? I'm the God of Winds – how can I have any credibility if I have no winds to be god of? You mortals simply have no idea."

"Have the rest come back? Are all the others in the cave? Why is Aura so important?"

There was a certain amount of silence, then the voice said rather stiffly, "Boreas came back. Zephyrus ... is thinking about it."

"So who's in the cave at the moment?"

Silence.

"No-one, right?"

Abruptly the Rachmaninov began again.

It was infuriating. On the one hand, I would really like a draught-free house. On the other hand, hounding someone out of a cupboard I didn't use much felt rather mean; and Aeolus was getting on my nerves. I felt also massively indignant at being involved in this absurd quarrel. All I'd done was live in a house with a cupboard.

The Rach stopped again. "All you have to do is tell her to leave. Tell her. Then it's no longer your problem." This time he was replaced by Bach which continued until I fell asleep, the dilemma still circling around in my mind.

Over the next three days, I left the radio off and stayed away from the cupboard, and two mugs, six pens, a box of biscuits and the steam iron disappeared. On the third day I bought a new bottle of gin. Once it was evening I turned the radio on and said, "Look, this isn't funny. You have no right to hide my things, or promise the imps theocratic immunity. You're causing me far more trouble than she is. I will *not* be bullied." The Chopin played on uninterrupted. I gave it half an hour, then went to the landing with the gin.

I opened the door; Aura was sitting on the floor, leaning against a side wall, playing patience with an old pack of cards advertising Woodbines. I offered her the gin, and she narrowed her eyes at me. "Where have you been?"

"That's a nice thing to say. I didn't have a libation. I only managed to get to Tesco this afternoon."

"Hm. Very well." She poured herself a large measure and graciously offered me back the bottle; I took a small tot in a glass I'd brought with me and said, "If I agree to let you stay here, is there anything you can do about the imps?"

"Hmph. There might be."

"Because at the moment I've got the worst of both worlds: imps and draughts."

She sniffed in answer.

"Aeolus says all I've got to do is tell you to go. He says then I'd have no more problem. Is that right?"

"You don't want to trust him, you know."

I took that as a yes. I said, "I don't. But then, can I trust you?"

"Well. Possibly."

"Because if I can, I've got a proposition."

She cocked a haughty eyebrow. "A *proposition*?"

"Yes. Why not? If you can get rid of the imps then you can stay. *If* you can stop *gusting* in the evenings and weekends. Blow all you like while I'm at work, *and* I'll bring you libations. How about it?"

She drank more gin, and stared thoughtfully into the glass, then gazed out of the door. Suddenly she stiffened and my head swung round to see what had caught her attention: six biros and three odd socks were whizzing past us on the landing, an inch or two above the floor.

"No shame!" she shouted. "No shame at all! He'll do anything! Promise them immunity, will he? We'll see about that." And a gale blew out of the cupboard, nearly knocking me over and blowing the socks and two of the biros on to the floor. The rest of the biros scurried off into the spare room.

I realised I'd left the radio on in my bedroom. The cultured, rather superior voice of Aeolus boomed out, "I will not tolerate insubordination!"

"Insubordination! Who do you think you are, Zeus? You gave us away, you know. You handed us over, and when that sailor let us out, that made us free breezes! You don't have any right to press me back to that bloody cave!" She glanced at me and said, "Lie down, or hold on to something."

It was the sort of tone you don't disobey. I lay down on the carpet and held on to the stair-post.

The blast that followed must have been quite high on the Beaufort scale. I was pressed against the bannister rail, with no chance of moving, and bombarded by random small objects as a storm of tiny, angry voices swept past. I shut my eyes and tensed. After some time the hail of small objects diminished, the voices were silent, and gradually the wind dropped, and everything became unnaturally still. When I was sure it wasn't going to start again I relaxed, let go of the stair-post, and cautiously stood up.

The house was not, as I'd expected, turned upside down. A lot of small things were out of place, but the furniture was still standing, and nothing was broken. I looked into the cupboard: Aura was very pale and looked as if she were asleep. I pulled the door to and tiptoed away into the bedroom, where the radio was ominously silent. I turned it off and unplugged it. I would have to sleep without it.

In the morning, the tooth brush, the mugs, the biscuits, and the iron were sitting in the middle of the kitchen table, beside a heap of pens, pencils, socks, and some notebooks and envelopes I hadn't missed. Since then, not so much as a paper-clip has mysteriously vanished. The house is draught-free at evenings and weekends, except that sometimes in the summer, if it's hot, a delightful cool breeze might drift through. Once a week I buy a bottle of libation for Aura; sometimes I leave it in the cupboard, sometimes we drink it together. I've taken up a couple of chairs. Danny hasn't rung, and I'm OK with that. The only annoyance is that I have to listen to the radio on the computer – if I turn the set on, every wavelength is full of an angry silence.

Contamination

Concrete and plastic and steel, as far as the eye could see, had eyes still existed. Concrete crumbled, plastic cracked, steel rusted, nothing else but one great clot of blood shed by the last mammal, all frozen in time when the atmosphere died, a million years of unfathomable cold ago.

Now they come from the other side of the galaxy, searching for land, seeding the planet, making a new atmosphere, making it warm, making it green. The blood, revived, seeking new flesh, seeking new bone, becoming what?

A creature of blood, a seeker of flesh, a seeker of bone.

They come, they settle, they build. The creature seeks their flesh, their bone, becomes their blood. Whoever they are, they become us; as they become us, they dream of concrete, of plastic, of steel.

The cycle begins again.

Eyes of God

"I don't hold with it," said Degla to the man with no nose, ears or lips, "all this disfiguring yourself to look more like a potato, to please the potato god. I mean, he's not stupid, is he? Surely he can tell the difference between you and a potato. Even I can tell the difference between you and a potato. And he's a god."

"Of course he can tell the difference," said Ilto. "It's to honour him, not confuse him. To honour the appearance of the potato, and thence to honour Gan."

"But the fact remains that you're not a potato. You're a person. Isn't there a god of people?"

"Of course there is. You know perfectly well. Asrin is god of people. But she has no power over the potato harvest. So we honour Gan in hopes that he will send us a good harvest."

"I see that. But if you're making yourself look more like a potato and less like a person, to honour Gan, doesn't that dishonour Asrin?"

"What?"

"I mean, I'd've thought the god of people would be offended that you prefer to look like a potato. Don't you risk some retaliation from her?"

"Don't be facetious."

"I'm not. I'm quite serious. Won't she be thinking, Huh, Ilto doesn't think looking like a person is good enough, he wants to look like a potato. I'll see he doesn't live long enough to eat his potato harvest."

"That's ridiculous. Each god accepts their own honour. I honour Asrin by feeding the poor, having children, and leaving an offering of potatoes at her shrine. That is the proper way to honour her; this is the way to honour Gan."

"Well, I still think it's theologically unsound."

The two were drinking chocolate on a terrace looking down the steep side of the mountain towards the canopy of the jungle. It was the feast of Matla, the corn god, a lesser god than Gan, but still honoured by three days of feasting, and last night's religious observances had been particularly strenuous. It was approaching noon and most people were awake by now, having a leisurely breakfast. A couple wandered on to the terrace, dressed in yellow and green; they looked as if they hadn't been home yet.

Ilto said, "Matla is also honoured by imitation. People dress as corn to win his favour."

"But only for the feast. They don't cut their bodies into ridges to look like an ear of corn all the time."

"Matla is a frivolous god. The worship of Gan is a serious business."

"Well," said Degla, "he will have to excuse me. I can't see it."

"It is not given to everyone to have a true devotion."

Degla decided to change the subject: "Are you going to the sacrifice tonight?"

"Of course. But goats and chickens are a poor sacrifice. As I say, Matla is a frivolous god."

"I don't want to offend even a frivolous god."

"And we shall not. But the proper sacrifice is a human heart."

"As long as it isn't mine."

"You are a frivolous person, Degla. I suppose it's only to be expected, you being a poet. You do not understand the serious business of devotion to the soil. If we were all poets, there would be nothing to eat."

"Ironic, though, don't you think, that we sacrifice

potatoes to the god of people, and people to the god of potatoes?"

"Hopelessly frivolous." Ilto smiled to show that he was not wholly disapproving, that he was fond of Degla anyway. "I must attend to some business. I'll see you at the temple tonight."

Ilto descended the steps at the back of the terrace and Degla watched him cycle across the square towards his offices. She shook her head. Ilto might think he was the serious one, but really, he had no idea. Degla's phone rang. She answered it and said, "Yes," at intervals for some minutes and eventually switched off. She sighed. The gods had only recently started to use the phone; it was probably an improvement on possessing people unexpectedly when they had a message to convey, but it did mean they talked a lot more than they used to. One thing stayed the same: you did what they … suggested … and no arguing.

Gan's main temple was a great pyramid in the city centre, next to the business district, but he had many small shrines, especially among the potato fields. It was to one of these that Degla cycled as the sun declined.

The shrine stood in a cleared area in the middle of a field. Degla laid down the bicycle at a respectful distance and walked carefully between the rows of plants. She stopped and knelt in the earth before the simple wooden pyramid and spoke. "Gan, the sustainer of our lives, firm and smooth and red and yellow and pink and blue, spirit of the sacred tuber, root and base of all goodness, speak with me now."

As she recited, a form rose out of the soil beside the shrine, a rounded brown shape that grew and grew until it was the height of a man, but knobbly and reddish, its skin covered with eyes and sprouts. Degla tried to decide which if any of the eyes were looking at her.

"Welcome, daughter," said a deep, earthy voice. "You have heard the future on the wind?"

"I've heard whispers, Lord Gan. Whispers from the soil, whispers in dreams. That a great famine is coming, that the food will wither in the ground, that a great blight will take it all, and people will starve. What can we do, Lord? Must we sacrifice more of our young people? Must you have blood? Is there anything we can do to avert this terrible fate?"

"No more blood." The dark, muddy voice was firm. "The fertilizing blood can do only so much. I'll tell you what you can do. And you must tell everyone. That's why I called you – you're a poet, you understand words, you can tell them, persuade them. Tell them this: they must abate their greed. They must stop over-farming, exhausting the soil. The gods of the earth are weary, they are worn out. And your farmers must diversify. Not only plant always the biggest, the most prolific, the cheapest to produce, but plant the large, the small, the late, the early, the yellow, the white, the red, the pink, and the purple. Rejoice in all my variety, honour me with love for all my fruits, not just with seeking always more money for less work. For that leads to famine and death. If they do these things the famine will not come. You must be my prophet and tell them these things."

"I will do it, Lord Gan. I don't know if they will listen."

"You will do a good job. If they won't listen then they will reap the harvest."

Lord Gan sank once more into the soil, and Degla went slowly home, wondering how she would put his words so that people would listen – listen to a frivolous poet. It wouldn't be easy.

*

Over the next few weeks she tried. She spoke, she wrote, she told people in prose and in verse. Some of them listened, some didn't. Many reviled her for blasphemy: how could a poet know more of the will of Gan than his priests and devotees who had suffered to do him honour? She was driven out of meetings, out of the public square. People threw stones and potatoes at her when she spoke, or as she passed in the street.

Then came the time for the feast of Gan and she knew what she had to do.

Before the ceremony that would culminate in the sacrifice, Degla climbed up the ziggurat and addressed the crowd. Many of them had heard her before and were mostly hostile; many had the sacred disfigurement, lacking ears, noses, lips. They were hardcore devotees of Gan, as they saw him. They would not have his ceremony marred by the ravings of a poet; they stood, staring at her, wondering if Gan himself would strike her down.

Degla bit her lip. The crowd was hard and angry below her on the steps. Her feet shook on the stones, but she kept her nerve and gave them Gan's message. She spoke with passion, with conviction, with inspiration

When she finished, a tall man spoke out of the silence: "We have heard you say all this before. But you are not of the faith, you have not served Gan as we have, your doctrines have no precedent. Gan is served by doing as we have always done. If you will not be silent and leave, we must give you to Gan."

"I cannot be silent," she replied. "It is the word of Gan that I tell you and this is the only way to save us all from starvation. The soil is worn out and we must change our ways."

"The word of Gan! Would Gan speak through a poet? Silence, woman, or go to Gan now!"

With a roar the crowd surged forward and two or three people grabbed her and forced her upward, to where the altar waited for the priest to make the sacrifice. The priest came forward, to protest that this was out of order, but the anger of the crowd intimidated him. He raised his arms, trying to speak above the shouting but made no move to intervene. The mutilated faces were ugly, distorted further by rage and hate.

Degla knew she was about to die. She tried to subdue her terror, at least to die with dignity. Her heart hammered but she focused on one thought: I can't withdraw what I said. It's true, and I mustn't deny it.

The grip on her arms was painful, the shouts in her ears were terrible. She took a deep breath and called, "Lord Gan! Witness to my truth!" The people who held her, forcing her towards the altar, were only more enraged. She struggled to stay on her feet as she was pushed from all sides, punched and slapped by those who could reach. Despite her resolve her heart hammered, her breath came short. The priest stood rigid by the altar, knowing the situation was out of his control.

They dragged Degla up the steps, catching her feet and legs against the stones, and came to the top of the ziggurat; at the sight of the altar they stopped, silenced. Over long minutes their silence spread, even to those who couldn't see what had caused it – the quality of the silence was so strong, the leaders so stunned by what they saw.

On the altar, ready for the sacrifice, beating slowly, was a potato in the exact form of a human heart.

Dead Men's Company

The sand burned the soles of their feet as they dragged the corpse up the beach. Heat beat in the air like a gong. The dead man was huge and wet and heavy, with rags of brine-soaked clothing clinging to his dark, heavily muscled body.

When they reached the tussocky grass of the dunes, the tall, scrawny man dropped the corpse's right arm and fell to his knees, gasping for breath. The short, stocky one, not out of breath, dropped the left arm and sat down, staring out to sea, his mouth a grim line. The scrawny one's gasps passed gradually into sobbing and he fell face down on the dune with his head on his arms.

Eventually the stocky one said, "Oh for heaven's sake, Lec, pull yourself together. We've got to bury him yet."

Lec pushed himself up into a sprawl, sniffing and wiping his face on his arm. "Do you think he'll stay buried? Will he come back again? I couldn't believe he washed up like that."

"Don't be soft. I just wish he hadn't had to die on our watch. Let's just get him buried."

"Sim, suppose the sand blows away and he comes back?"

"With any luck he'll be unrecognisable by then. As long as Kamal doesn't know he's dead, it doesn't matter, does it?"

It took a long time to dig the grave with their hands and knives, but they dared not go back for spades or mattocks. If anyone asked what they were doing —

At last the hole was big enough. Their hands were

bleeding; sweat streamed into their eyes, down their bodies; sand chafed in their clothes, in the backs of their knees. They hauled the half-dried body of Manero to the edge of the hole. Then Sim said, "Stop a minute."

"What?"

Sim rummaged at the corpse's waist; he straightened with a laugh, his hand clasped around a sodden leather pouch. Lec's eyes widened.

"Strapped under his breeches," said Sim with a grin. He pulled open the mouth of the pouch and gasped.

Lec leaned forward and stared – the pouch was full as it would hold with gold coins. They gazed at the money for a long time, then gazed at each other.

"Where did he get it?" whispered Lec.

Sim shrugged. "Saved it? Robbed someone? Who cares? He doesn't need it any more. It's *ours*."

"*No!* You can't – we can't – we can't do that!"

"Why not? What else should we do? Bury it?"

"I don't know. But – looting a corpse, Sim – they hang you for that."

"They do in the army. We're not *in* the army now. Right?"

"Uh."

"Lec, this is our future. This is our ticket out of here, away from Kamal. No more plantation work. No more dirt pay. No more kicks from the likes of Manero. What's the *problem*, boy?"

The thin man shook his head. His guts knotted at the thought of Kamal, at the thought of being found with Manero's money...

"What shall we do, though, Sim? When we go back –"

"We're not *going* back."

"Not–?"

"What do you want to go back for, Lec? What is there

to go back for? Your mother's portrait? Letters from your sweetheart?"

"You know I don't have stuff like that. But ... I don't know. There's my boots and my good suit—"

"Lec, the first thing we're going to do is buy a better suit and pair of boots than you ever had in your life."

"Where? Where are we going?"

"We're going to Port Hell."

"Oh. Oh."

"Kamal will never expect to find us there, even if he looks for us. We can get good clothes and food and liquor and women, and then – there's ships sail from Port Hell. We can go anywhere."

"Oh. Yes, liquor and women ... I don't know..."

"Of course you want liquor and women. Everyone does."

"But – we don't want to spend all the money at once, Sim."

"Of course we shan't. Now come on, let's get this son of a dog buried and get out of here."

*

By the time they had tumbled Manero into the hole and shoved the sand back to cover him the sun was low, but at the end of the long walk Port Hell was still wide open and blazing with light. Before they came down from the dunes, Sim transferred a little of Manero's money to their pockets and stowed the pouch inside his shirt. "No point in *inviting* robbers," he said.

They walked warily past the bars and brothels and pawnshops by the docks, and not till they came into the better part of town did Sim start looking in shop windows. They bought shirts and jackets, breeches and underwear, boots and hats and belts. Lec said, "Are you sure we need all this?"

"Sure we do. We're gentlemen of leisure now and we're going to live like it. Do you know where we're going tonight? The Port Hell Hotel."

"What! We can't afford to stay there, can we? Even with – what we've got."

"For one night we can. I've wanted to drink with the gentry for a long time and now we're going to do it."

*

At first Lec was impressed with the bar of the Port Hell Hotel. The gilt, the mirrors, the upholstered chairs, the smell of cigars, the flashily dressed customers, the price of the drinks. About the third round he became uncomfortably aware of the painted smiles on the painted faces of the bar girls, the despair in the empty eyes of the man who collected the glasses, the scrawny woman who emptied the ashtrays and wiped the tables with a fixed expression of malevolent misery.

He said, "I'm not sure I like this place, Sim."

"Oh rubbish. Have another drink."

"I'd rather have something to eat."

Sim snorted but ordered food; the man with the empty eyes brought a plate of fried octopus, and some slightly stale bread.

"Sim," said Lec, "I can't help thinking –"

"Well try harder."

"No … but if Kamal finds out Manero's dead he's bound to think we killed him."

"That's why we buried him, isn't it? If no-one knows he's dead they can't think we killed him."

"We didn't kill him, did we?"

"For gut's sake! Of course we didn't kill him. He died of an apoplectic, just like my old granddad."

"But he had the apoplectic because he found us skiving off."

"That was his problem. He shouldn't have drunk so much. Have some more rum."

Lec continued to brood glumly as he chewed his octopus.

The noise and cigar smoke increased in volume; the malevolence on the face of the scrawny woman increased in intensity. One of the painted bar girls brought another round of drinks; as she bent over, the closeness of her high-corseted, low-necked dress caused both men to feel that their new breeches were rather too tight. A whisper in her ear from Sim got him nothing but a dirty look. When she had gone, Sim belched and farted and said, "You know, when this money runs out—"

"Which it will soon, at these prices."

"—*when* the money runs out, what we need is to be the playthings of a rich woman."

"Why?" said Lec.

"Why? Why not? You get well fed, well dressed, you live in a nice house, and all you have to do for it is a bit of—" he made a crude gesture. "What's not to like?"

"Well ... she might be ugly."

"*So close your eyes.*"

*

Despite the clean and very expensive bed in the hotel, Lec didn't sleep well. He tossed and turned, got up three times to use the chamber pot, and was haunted by nightmares.

In the morning he said to Sim, who had slept like a log and snored like a band saw, "Sim, I dreamed that Manero got up out of his grave and came after us, wanting his money back."

"So? You shouldn't have ate so much octopus."

"But look, suppose *he* thinks we killed him? Suppose he thinks, If it hadn't of been for those two, I wouldn't have had an apoplectic, and then they took my money, and he comes after us for revenge?"

"For gut's sake. Dead men don't come out of their graves."

"Yes they do."

"What?"

"When I was in Port Enfer, they talked about a pirate ship with a female captain, and all the crew were dead men who'd been called up out of their graves."

"That's a sailor's tale, Lec. They make them up in the long watches when there's nothing to do, to frighten the cabin boys."

"I dunno. I want to go and see."

"What? See what?"

"Where we buried Manero. See if he's still there."

"Look – oh, all right! All right, go if it'll make you happy."

"I'm not going on me own. Suppose he's waiting for me?"

*

"It wasn't here. This is just where some animal's been digging. It must have been further along."

"It was here. Look, there's a bit of his coat. He's dug his way out and come after us."

Sim was sufficiently unnerved to say, "Well, all right. We want to get away from here anyway. We'll get a passage on the next ship that's sailing. He's not going to swim after us, is he?"

"I dunno. He might."

*

On their way back they looked out from the headland. There was only one ship in the bay. It was dead black, with a black flag, and eight black sails.

"Don't know if I fancy a passage on that," said Sim.

"I dunno," said Lec, "we could try."
"Let's go and get some food," said Sim, "and a drink."

*

The Port Hell Hotel was less crowded at midday and looked slightly seedy with sunlight on it. The scrawny woman was sweeping the floor. She glared at them. They had curry goat and beer, and more beer; the place started to fill up, and Lec was beginning to relax a bit. Then he looked up as the door opened and gave a kind of strangled squeal, and said, "Oh damn."

"What?"

"I've wet meself."

"What?"

"Look – there in the doorway. Look."

Sim looked. It was Manero, clothes in rags, still slightly damp, shedding sand, looking very dead. He was talking – or trying to talk – to the woman who was sweeping the floor; she stared at him with contempt. The conversation had fallen quiet around him. As people noticed him they edged away and looked towards the exit.

Sim gave a throttled squawk and made to rise. He reached in his pocket, carefully, took out money, and left enough on the table to cover their bill. The last thing they wanted was to attract attention. Then they got up and retreated behind an ornamental pillar.

They were unfortunately a long way from the door and would have to cross Manero's line of vision to reach it. They retreated further and were standing behind a decorative screen when the door opened again.

This time it was a crowd that entered, and through the door at the far end of the bar as well. Some were wearing sea-boots and long, full-skirted coats, and carried cutlasses and pistols. Lec thought they were all women. Probably. The rest wore clothing in rags – and bodies much the same; flesh hung in tatters, their bones showed through, yellow and dry. They looked much deader than Manero.

Lec moaned.

"*What?*" squawked Sim under his breath.

"It's the crew of the black ship. It's the pirates I told you about."

"Oh damn."

"What?"

"I've wet meself too, now."

"We're dead men, Sim. We're dead."

"Doesn't look like the pay and conditions are much good either."

There was nowhere further to retreat. They stood behind the screen, trying to breathe silently.

The conversation, which had risen again since Manero's entrance, had now stopped completely. Everyone watched the pirates, nervously gulping drinks and trying foolishly to edge purses and jewellery out of sight, waiting for the invaders to move.

The woman who had led them in was tall and dark, wide-shouldered, with one blazing green eye, and a scar that began at the hairline of her left temple, reappeared below the black silk eye patch, and ended just above the corner of her mouth.

A youngish man who was standing at the bar, rather dandified, with diamond studs in his shirt and ears, gold rings on his fingers, and far too much wine in his bloodstream, raised a supercilious eyebrow. "Duelling scar?" he asked.

She shook her head. "Axe," she said, and ordered a bottle of rum. With it in her hand she turned and scanned the room. Lec thought she caught the eye of the woman sweeping the floor, and that the woman sweeping the floor nodded.

The one-eyed woman took a long drink of rum. Some of the other women took drinks; a few people began to relax a little, murmur conversation.

The scarred woman looked across the room. "Hey! Manero!"

"Swan! I was looking for you." His voice was low and hollow.

"You dead, man?"

"I am."

"Told you, you shouldn't lose your temper so much. Burst a blood vessel by the look of you. Want to join us?"

"Sure."

She gave him the bottle, and the dead man took a long swig of rum. He handed the bottle back; she stood drinking and surveying the room. She made a gesture and some of the other women began moving round, staring at the stout and prosperous patrons of the Port Hell Hotel, sometimes pinching a cheek or a bicep.

Lec and Sim heard the one-eyed woman, as she turned to the dandified man, say, "You see, there's one thing our crew can't do for us, being dead. We have to refill the harem when we get the chance – shame to waste any. But they've got to be young and strong." She looked him up and down; "You're not so bad. But you're not that way inclined, are you? Pity."

He made a noise like a man with a chicken bone stuck in his throat, and dropped his drink.

The other women came back shaking their heads. The one-eyed woman sighed, finished the bottle of rum, looked once more towards the woman with the broom and raised her hand. The women and the dead men moved out among the customers, drawing knives, and began cutting throats.

Lec sat in a tight huddle on the floor, his head wrapped

in his arms. Sim crouched beside him. As people fought to get away, the screen was knocked over but it still covered the two. They waited for the feel of a knife edge on their necks as the room filled with screams and harsh laughter.

In a few minutes the room was quiet, the smell vile. Lec was trying to remember how to pray.

The screen was lifted off and Manero's voice said, "Hey! It's you two!" He lifted them with one hand on the neck of each. "I ought to be angry with you little rats, but what the hell. Being dead isn't as bad as I thought. At least I don't have to work for Kamal any more. Oh, the money? That's all right – let Swan have it. I stole it anyway." He roared with laughter. "Hey, Swan! There's two here I know. You want to keep them? They're not idle rich swabs like those others – even if they did take my money, hey?"

The one-eyed woman turned her attention from those who were relieving the bodies of valuables, and walked over. She looked them up and down, pinched their muscles, turned their heads this way and that, looked at their teeth. The cleaning woman joined them – she had swapped her broom for a cutlass. The woman with the scar suddenly shot out a hand and grabbed Lec between the legs, at which he squealed. She gave a deep rasping laugh and did the same to Sim. Although he was braced for it he caught his breath; her hand was like iron.

"They've both got what it takes," she said. "This one's got a bit of muscle but he's ugly. That one could be pretty if he was cleaned up a bit, but he's just a piece of string. What do you think, Jen?"

The cleaning woman laughed. "Bring 'em if you want, Swan."

The scarred woman grinned at them. "Ready for a fate worse than death, boys?"

Lec gaped in horror; Sim cleared his throat, and said, "We're your men, Madam. If we change our minds we can always die later."

As they were marched out of the slaughterhouse at the point of a cutlass, Sim whispered, "Cheer up. We're the playthings of rich women. What's the problem?"

"They're ugly. And they'll kill us if we can't get it up."

"Well then, close your eyes and think of whatever it takes. If they kill us they'll take us on the crew, and that'll be hard work."

*

Over the next few weeks, Lec had to admit that it was probably better than being dead. He usually went to sleep at night too tired to think, and when he watched Manero and the other dead men swabbing decks and hauling ropes he didn't really envy them. He had a soft bed, and good clothes, plenty of food to keep his strength up – mostly lobscouse and ship's biscuit, but he'd eaten worse, and sometimes there was dried fruit or fish to vary the menu – and he was washed every day. He didn't often see Sim or the other handful of men in the harem.

Swan visited him nearly every night – she seemed to have taken a fancy to him. He decided that Sim was right: if he closed his eyes it was not hard to think of her as beautiful and alluring. Particularly when she was in a good mood and had brought a couple of bottles of port to bed, to share alike.

Several times they chased down a merchant ship and fired her a broadside or two; sometimes the merchant tried to run but the black ship was fast, with or without a wind – someone said the draught from the fires of hell filled her sails. The result was always the same: the pirate crew would grapple the merchant, swarm over her and slaughter everyone on board – unless there was a strong young man or so that the pirates took a fancy to. The dead crew had the advantage, of course, in that they could not be killed, although if an adversary was lucky enough to cut off a crewman's sword arm he stood a fighting chance.

During a fight, the men of the harem were kept under hatches, and only too glad of it, while the screaming and bloodshed went on overhead. Afterwards, with the officers drunk on action, was another matter.

When Sim and Lec had been at sea three or four weeks the men of the harem were enjoying a rare afternoon on deck with pipes and conversation. They were allowed this from time to time when things were quiet. The night before had been particularly drunken, when a captured merchantman had proved to be carrying a cargo of old brandy, and no-one had the energy to require their services today. The black sails were full; there was little sound beyond the creak of the rigging and the rattle of dead men playing dice amidships. Lec and Sim were leaning against the rail, staring mindlessly out to sea; they heard a step behind them, and Manero said, "Well, lads? How are you liking it?"

Manero was not looking any better; he was beginning to come to pieces a little and had lost an ear and a couple of fingers in one of the fights.

"Well enough," said Sim. "How about you?"

"It's not what I'd hoped. They work us hard. The fighting's good – that's always good – but swabbing the decks is dull work. Dull work. And I don't seem to enjoy drinking half so well now I'm dead. To tell the truth..."

"Well?"

"Can I trust you lads?"

"I shouldn't think so," said Lec. "Why should you? You only ever clouted us and whipped us when you were alive, and when you were dead we stole your money.

Why should you trust us?"

"That's true. That's true enough. The fact is, though, we need someone living to help us. And if it came off, you'd have your freedom."

"If what came off? Help with what?"

"Just a moment," said Sim, "don't tell us any more, Manero. If you're talking about what I think you're talking about, we don't want to know. We're not fighting men – as you might have gathered – and we don't want to know about anything that might be bad for our health."

"Oh, you wouldn't have to do any fighting. We'd do all that."

There was a pause, then Sim said, "Go on."

"We've had enough, see? Just because we're dead, we don't have to like being ordered about, doing all the dirty work. We want the chance to enjoy ourselves – so far as we can. Why not? What have we got to lose, after all? We can't be killed."

"You're talking about mutiny," said Sim in a low voice.

"Aye, so I am. I'm not afraid of the word. Are you with us? You've more to lose, I allow that; but you've more to gain. Your freedom, your manhood. You can win your lives back."

"What do you need us for?" asked Lec.

"That's straight talking," said Manero. "I'll tell you. You know us dead men ain't allowed below. You lads can come and go. We need the key of the powder magazine."

Lec thought about it, then shook his head. "I'm alive," he said, "and I want to stay that way. No offence. It's too chancy."

Manero looked at Sim. "Are you yellow, too? Would you sooner live under a woman's foot than take a chance?"

Sim shifted his feet. Being the plaything of a rich

woman was proving to have its drawbacks, but his natural reaction was the same as Lec's. The accusation of cowardice rankled, though. He moved his shoulders uneasily. "I'll do it if I can," he said at last. "I can't promise. They keep a pretty sharp eye on us."

Manero nodded. "Good man. What about you?" he turned to Lec. "Will you go squealing to your mistress?"

"No," said Lec, "not if Sim's in with you. In any case, I doubt she'd believe me. But I think you're a pack of fools. It won't work."

Manero laughed and strode off.

Sim said, "Why shouldn't it work?"

"I'm not clever," said Lec, "but neither is Manero. Some of those women are damned clever. If this would work, it would've happened before."

"No," said Sim. "Manero's the first one to have the gumption to try it. The others have been dead too long."

"Get below! Get below, damn you!" The thin woman from the hotel bellowed at them. "There's a storm blowing up! Hey, you lubbers! Lay aloft and take in t'garns, reef your fore and main! Take in canvas, damn your eyes! You there, batten down the hatches!"

The sky behind the ship was black; they ran for the companion way.

The storm was on them in minutes. The ship pitched and rolled and Lec, in his bunk, felt for the first time desperately seasick and lost all interest in the outside world. The rest of the day and most of the night they were flung up and down, back and forth, on the heaving sea. Lec knew only that the porthole was sometimes underwater, sometimes pointing at the sky, and he wished he were dead. When the storm blew itself out towards morning he fell into an uneasy sleep.

He was woken as if by a thunderclap. He looked

around wildly; after a few moments he realised that sunlight was flooding through the porthole, the ship was on an even keel, and the noise from above was pistol shots. Manero had begun his mutiny.

Reluctantly, torn between fears, choosing, with a wince, the known over the unknown, Lec opened the cabin door and scrambled up the companion way. He put his head cautiously up through the hatchway and looked about.

The deck swarmed with fighting men and women, the air rang with yells and shots. The hatchway was half hidden behind a stack of casks and Lec emerged hesitantly out on deck and crouched.

A few feet away Swan, with her back to him, was fighting two dead crewmen with cutlass and dagger. A movement caught Lec's eyes; to one side of him another crewman was levelling a pistol at Swan's back. Before he knew what he was doing Lec lunged and knocked the man's arm up. The pistol went flying; the dead man came for him with a yell. Lec dodged back behind the casks and Swan, having disarmed both her opponents in time to turn as the pistol hit the planking, slashed off the crewman's head. She flashed Lec a frown then plunged forward across the deck.

Lec twisted sharply at a noise behind him; it was Sim scuttling into the shelter of the casks. He knelt, gasping for breath, then said, "Gut's sake! What did you do that for?"

"I – I don't know. It sort of happened."

"You're not on their side, are you? Just because they're women, they're not going to turn out to be good at heart. Don't get soft."

"Oh hell, I know. She's brutal, ruthless and bloodthirsty. But I kind of like that."

A knot of fighting surged towards them and they ducked. They heard the woman from the hotel scream,

"Swan, this is all your fault, you lousy swab, bringing that bastard Manero aboard."

The fighting rolled away again. There was a noise behind them, a smothered expletive and the cocking of a pistol.

Manero stood there, aiming point-blank at Sim's chest. He pulled the trigger but there was only a click as the piece missed fire. With a howl he flung it down, swapped the cutlass to his other hand and lunged. Sim yelled and sprinted across the deck. Lec moved around the casks, dodging Manero's blade —

"What did you do that for?" he cried. "He was on your side, he helped you!"

"Can't have living and dead in the same crew – don't mix. Want to join us? We'll take you on the account as soon as you're dead."

"The hell you will!" Lec sidestepped, retreated, the steel slashing close to his belly. He turned and ran, swerving between bodies, living and dead, towards one of the ship's boats which should be swinging on the davits – but the boat was gone. He leapt for the rail and threw himself out as far as he could. By great good luck he avoided being splatted on the gun ports. As he struck the blue water and sank down and down, he remembered that he couldn't swim. Still, drowning was better than working for Manero again. The momentum of his plunge exhausted, he began to rise and as his head broke the surface, something grabbed his hair. He screamed, getting a mouthful of sea, and then something grabbed the scruff of his neck and hauled him up. He rolled over the gunwale of a small boat, lay gasping for a moment, crawled to the side and threw up, then scrambled back to sit on the stern thwart. In the bow Swan was vigorously plying the oars, pulling away from the black ship.

"What—?" he said. "Why—?"

"I shan't be popular there, whoever wins," she said. "Jen blames me for bringing Manero aboard. Dammit, I didn't know he was such a damn troublemaker. His grandmother was a loa, you see, an invisible, and he can't die quietly like other people... Oh, you mean why did I haul you out of the briny?" The boat clove the water for some distance before she said, "I don't know why you saved my life back there, lad, but I'll not be beholden to a dead man. We're quits now. And you can steer and help row. No sense your going to Davy Jones if you can be useful. With luck, we might make landfall before we die of thirst."

She grinned ferociously and he smiled weakly back. Somehow, it had never crossed his mind that being the plaything of a rich woman would involve so much senseless violence and sudden death. The noise behind them died away. The sun slipped down the sky throwing his shadow across the water. The wind swung round behind them and Swan put up the oars. Reaching down under the thwarts she pulled out a short mast, which she set up in the bows.

As a small black lugsail quivered and caught the breeze Swan consulted a compass on a thong about her neck. She took it off and passed it over. "East by south-east," she said.

Lec put his hand to the tiller. "East by south-east it is."

Meeting at the Silver Dollar

It was early, too early for the whores and gamblers to be awake, but one man sat in the Silver Dollar saloon, watching the door, holding a silver dollar, throwing it up and catching it. He wore an overcoat, it being a cold day, but as his arm moved you could see a silver star pinned to his vest. There was a bottle of whiskey on the table in front of him but he was drinking coffee.

Tucson Charlie, the bartender, was sweeping the floor and gradually lifting all the chairs down and settling them around the tables. He glanced round frequently at the door and at the man with the star.

Charlie had reached the back of the room when a figure appeared at the swing doors. The man with the star looked up, his hand dropping the dollar on the table and moving to his side; but he halted the movement when he saw the one who walked in.

Not even a man, he thought, a boy; hardly growing a beard yet. Seventeen or so? But sharply dressed, and the Colt that hung from his hip was business-like. The boy pushed open the swing doors, stepped through and stood pat. The man with the star looked him up and down.

The boy said, "Are you looking at me, mister?"

"Ain't no-one else here, boy. No offence. I'm waiting for someone but you ain't the one I'm waiting for. Sit down; take a drink."

Charlie, looking nervous, brought over a couple of glasses. The boy hesitated, then sat, keeping the chair back a little from the table, hand hovering over his gun.

The man with the star poured two glasses of whiskey,

pushed one across the chipped polish of the table. The boy took it, sipped the rough liquor. He seemed to be used to drinking. He took another sip and said, "Who are you waiting for?"

"Feller called Dan Morris. And I have to tell you, son, if he turns up, things are likely to get lively around here."

"I guess I ain't afraid of that. And don't call me son. I'm nineteen – I'm a man."

"Well, son, you'll have to forgive me, but I'm forty six and you sure look more like a boy to me. Now don't get riled up. I can see you know how to handle yourself. Where you from? If'n you don't mind my asking."

"I'm from West Texas. Concho County."

"Uh-huh. You're a long way from home."

"Had to leave. I killed a man in a fight. But it suits me; I'm aiming to see the world, make me some money, see something of life."

"Yeah? You go round talking about killing people and wearing that pistol the way you do, you're more likely to see something of death."

"Not me. Why, I'm the fastest gun in Concho County."

"Is that right? Is that how you killed that feller, with a gun?"

"Yes sir. He insulted my sister and I called him out. He hadn't hardly cleared leather when I shot him."

"How many men you killed, altogether?"

"Uh – just the one, so far. Why?"

"Well, you got time to stop. Couple more, that's it: you have to go on."

"Why should I want to stop? I mean, I ain't a murderer but there's people out there – bad people – that need stopping, even if I have to kill them."

The man with the badge shook his head. He'd heard it so many times before, from so many men and boys that were out there now in Boot Hill, or on their way there. He sighed. "So, son – mister – what you doing here, in my town?" He moved his arm as he said it and the boy caught sight of the badge on his vest.

The boy sat up a little straighter. "Are you the sheriff?"

"Guess I am."

"Well – I'm sorry – I guess I've been talking out of turn a little. But that guy I shot, it was a fair fight. I mean, I'm not wanted. I'm not on the run. Only thing was, his folks was after me and I had to clear out for a while. So I figured it was a good chance to get out and see something of the world. You know what I mean? Okay. So, what am I doing in your town? I'm looking for a man named Frank Davis."

The sheriff was very still for a moment, then he said, "Yeah? So who's Frank Davis and why do you want to find him?"

"You mean you never heard of Frank Davis? I thought everyone'd know Frank Davis. Why, he's my hero. He faced down the Cosker gang and beat them single-handed. He cleaned up Grover with just one old man and a boy. He's brought the law to half the towns in the West. I can't believe you never heard of him!" The boy heard the barman behind him give a kind of snort, and he narrowed his eyes at the man with the star; "You have heard of him. You're just making fun of me."

"I wouldn't do that, son. But you're wrong, Frank Davis ain't no hero. And I ought to know."

"Why? How would you know? Who are you?"

The barman laughed and the man with the star said, "I'm Frank Davis."

The boy gaped. "You – you're – you're Frank Davis?"

"Uh-huh. And I ain't no hero. You want to know the truth? I faced the Coskers single-handed – sure. With six men backing me up from the roof of the hotel and the church and the window over the dry goods store. I cleaned up Grover – but it was pretty clean already, most of the riff-raff had moved on when the silver ran out. As for the law – that's my job, boy. I'm paid for it and I do it. Dan Morris is coming to get me because I arrested him for bank robbery, and he's just done four years in the State prison. If he draws on me I'll kill him or he'll kill me, but the world won't be a better place, either way —

"I'm not a hero, boy. If I ever had any interest in being a hero I left it with my brother under the peach trees at Shiloh. You understand me?"

"You were a soldier?"

"Sure I was. And let me tell you, a soldier ain't a hero. A soldier's just a damn fool."

"I can't believe that."

"A soldier's a man that goes out to kill or get killed for someone else's idea. A lawman goes out to get killed for wages. Neither of them is a hero. A hero's a man that raises crops or cattle, and marries a decent woman and raises kids, and feeds them and teaches them right from wrong. If there were more heroes like that, there wouldn't be no need for soldiers and lawmen. Hear what I'm telling you, son?"

"I hear you, Mr Davis. But – I guess I don't quite see it that way. Seems to me there's always going to be bad men and someone has to stand up against them."

"That's a fact. But it ain't nothing to be proud of. And it ain't something to hanker after. Once you're up there, standing against them, you're a target for the rest of your life. You understand that? You're a hero today, maybe, but when the town quietens down and gets respectable, and they pull down the whorehouse and build a church — Charlie, what you sniggering at?"

"Pull down the whorehouse? No town ever gets that respectable."

"Well, they move it out of town, then. Will you shut up? I'm trying to save this kid's life. OK, so they get respectable and then they realise they've got this gunslinger cluttering up the sheriff's office, making the place look untidy, and they start hinting that there's other towns need cleaning up, sheriff, no offence, and eventually they run you out of town. That's why I keep moving on. Not because I have some divine mission to bring law to the West – I just keep getting run out of town. That ain't no way to live, boy."

"I – I dunno, Mr Davis. I don't guess I'm cut out for farming, and it ain't much life being a ranch hand. I hear what you're saying, but – hell, I'm good with a gun. There's got to be some way to use that."

"Well, I sure don't know any way to use being good with a handgun that doesn't involve shooting people. And I've shot a lot of people, and I don't say any of 'em was much loss, but then again, what have I got to show for it? If Dan Morris kills me today there won't be nothing left behind, except a few dime novel stories that don't tell the truth."

"But he ain't going to kill you, Mr Davis. You're the best there is."

"Look, boy, if you tell anyone this, I'll deny it: I'm slowing down. That's the other thing that happens – you slow down. You can't help it. Unless you die young, you get old. My reactions are slowing, my hand just plumb don't move like it used to. Maybe I'll kill Dan. And maybe he'll kill me. If I get lucky today, maybe I won't the next time. You follow me? Sooner or later, someone's going to be quicker. You just wait for that time. And mostly you wait on your own. I tell you, boy, get a job on a cattle drive or go out prospecting or, hell, even get a job tending bar. But don't try getting into the hero business. It don't pay near as well as you think."

"Hell, Mr Davis, I don't know what to say. I still think you're a damn fine man, but – hell – "

"And don't cuss so much. You're too young."

"What? Uh – "

Charlie said, "He don't like to hear people cuss. It's the way his ma brought him up."

"Shut up, Charlie."

The boy stammered a bit, then said, "Look, Mr Davis, seems to me if what you're saying is true, anyone might be faster than you. Anyone. Even me."

The sheriff's eyes narrowed. "You want to try it, boy? Cos I tell you, the fastest gun in Concho County ain't necessarily the fastest gun anywhere else. And I ain't slowed down that much."

"Uh – he – heck no, Mr Davis. I didn't mean that!"

"You was thinking it though. You was thinking, Hell, if that's true, if I can out-gun my hero, don't that make me a hero? Wasn't you, son?" He sounded more sad than angry.

The boy reddened. "I wouldn't do that, Mr Davis. I – I respect you. And I see what you're doing. You reckon to talk me out of what I'm set on because, well, I guess you ain't sure I've got what it takes. But I have. I have got what it takes. I know it'll mean always having to be the best, having to watch my back, never resting. But I'm willing to do that, if I can make the world safer and more decent."

"You ain't listening," said the sheriff. "It don't make the world any safer or more decent. What makes a town, and the world, decent, is if enough of the folks in it want it to be decent. Ain't a thing a man with a gun can do about that. And without that, don't matter how many bad hombres you send to meet their maker, there'll always be just as many to take their place. Do you understand now?"

Charlie said, "Give it up, son. He's got twenty-five years start on you in the arguing business. And he's right. If people ain't behind the law, it can't work; and if they are, it shouldn't need six-guns to back it up. Of course, it doesn't always actually work out that way but that's sure the way to bet. You might make a difference or you might not, but you'll never know and you'll never be thanked, even if you did."

"Charlie, will you let me do this my way? Being disillusioned by your hero is one thing; being disillusioned by a bartender is just damned embarrassing." The boy tried to suppress a grin and the sheriff said, "He's right about the last bit. You'll never know if you made things better or worse, or made no difference; and you sure as hell won't get any gratitude."

"I ain't looking for gratitude," the boy protested, taking another drink of whiskey to mask his confusion. "But when you say you never know if you made things better or worse – is that true?"

"True for me, true for most people I know. Listen, son, if you really want to be rootless all your life, never have a wife and kids to come home to, never have a place to call home, never to have a friend you know you can trust, always tell your troubles to bartenders because they're the only people who'll listen, because listening is their job – What is it, Charlie?"

"I hear the noon train coming in, sheriff. The train Dan Morris'll most likely be on."

"Thanks, Charlie. Listen, son, you better clear out. You don't want to be caught in the cross-fire –"

"Look out!"

The boy's voice, the crash of glass, the sound of two shots, and a second, smaller crash, came so hard upon each other they seemed like just one sound. Then the boy was on his feet. Charlie was coming up from under the bar with a shotgun, glancing at his shattered mirror. Frank Davis was half turned in his chair and a man was lying bleeding in the gap of a broken window at the side of the room. The sheriff stood up and walked across the bar.

Charlie said, "Might be more of them outside," and kept the shotgun trained on the window, with an eye also to the swing doors.

The sheriff looked out of the window, then bent to the man lying across the sill, his hand, still holding the gun, hanging down on the floor, his head against the wall, his legs grotesquely still in the street. "It's Dan Morris and he's dead." He looked out once more. "Looks like he was alone. Boy—" he turned around "—I take it back. You are good."

The boy stood still, his face dead white, the six-gun still in his hand. "Uh. Thank you. He – I just saw him as he—"

"You saved my life." The sheriff's voice was flat, a little bleak. "I honestly don't know if I'm glad or sorry."

"Yeah. I mean – I didn't think. It just happened."

Charlie the bartender said, "There'll be people here soon. What are we going to tell them?"

The sheriff and the boy looked at each other.

Charlie went on: "If Frank Davis shot Dan Morris, that ain't news. That's what everyone expects. If a Texan boy no-one's heard of shot Dan Morris and saved Frank Davis's life, that's news. Either of you want to be news?"

There was a silence that lasted half a minute and felt like half a lifetime. The sheriff said, "I guess it has to be up to you, boy. Maybe I'm wrong, after all, and this is what you should be doing."

The boy shook his head violently. "No. No, I – hell, I feel sick. I mean, I'm glad I saved your life, Mr Davis, even if you're not. But I don't … I don't want to make my living shooting strangers. That's just … you're right, that ain't no way to live." He holstered his gun, sat down, and took another slug of whiskey.

The sheriff said, "Charlie, did you see what happened?"

"Not me, sheriff, I didn't see a thing. My eyesight's so bad I never do, you know that. I'm deaf, too."

There were people, now, at the doors, looking over, sussing out the situation. The first to enter was the undertaker, Nathan Black.

"Sheriff. You got me another customer?"

"That's right, Nath. Dan Morris got what he was looking for."

"Reckon he slipped off the train early and stole a horse. Figured he'd fool you, take you by surprise. Ed saw him sneaking up the side of the saloon, but there wasn't nothing we could do."

"I guess there never is. Take him away, Nath, bury him proper. The town'll have to foot the bill."

"Ain't no sneaking up on you, sheriff. You're a real hero."

"Sure. Sure I am, Nathan. Take him away. And get someone to come fix that window, there's a hell of a draught."

Story Notes

I grew up reading MR James and Conan Doyle, among others, but looking at this lot my main influences seem to be old movies and traditional folk songs.

"Cave Arborem" (*Beware of the Tree*, obviously), was mentioned in Ellen Datlow's long list of Best Horror, which was highly gratifying. It is what it is. Trees can be uncanny.

"Music in the Bone" is a tale that comes from a traditional ballad, the one where the rejected older sister pushes the younger in the river, and when the body's fished out a minstrel makes a harp of her breastbone, which then accuses the murderer. I have mangled it out of all recognition I'm afraid. I blame Pyewackett for this one – their version of the song haunted me for years.

"The Seal Songs" was written in the 1970s, long before I ever went to the Hebrides, based on reading a book on life on Barra in the 1930s, although the story is set in the 1950s and on an imaginary Hebridean island. Barra and South Uist are predominantly Catholic, which is why Ewan and his father go to Mass. I have been to Barra, now, and climbed an almost vertical path to the church of Our Lady, Star of the Sea, and very beautiful it is. I didn't hear the seals sing, but I've met people who have.

I wrote "Amenities" when I was watching a cricket match, and being superstitious – as one gets watching sport – I started to feel that when I concentrated too hard the team I was supporting lost wickets. So I tried to think about something else and began this story in a stream-of-consciousness sort of way, which is often how I write anyway.

"Sunlight in Spelling" is another early effort. It's sort of science fiction, although my dystopian future isn't very scientific. The idea of the sun being completely obscured came from a visit to Los Angeles, which from a distance was visibly enveloped in brown air.

"Disposal of the Body" – this is a bit embarrassing. I was trying to get back into writing after a long gap and finding my stories were considered old-hat and predictable. I read a couple of recently published horror anthologies and tried to write something with a similar feel, that would produce a similar feeling (in me) of "What the hell was that all about?" This was the result. I have a few ideas of what may be going on, but nothing concrete...

"Out of Season" comes of spending a lot of time at traditional festivals in Cornwall. The effect of a tall hobby horse with a horse's skull, accompanied by a group of musicians playing Bodmin Riding, entering unexpectedly into a darkened room, is considerable.

"Washing of the Waters" is a kind of phantasmagoric montage of two or three traditional ballads. Of course in the originals everyone dies.

"Saxophony" – I wanted to call it *Sax in the City*, but the editor wasn't impressed. Have you ever met someone and felt very strongly that you know them, although it's quite clear that you don't? And you start wondering, Do they just remind you of someone, or did you know them in a previous life, or what? This is about that feeling. And I've always had a thing about saxophone players.

"Looking Glass" was written quite quickly for a Hallowe'en special. I hope it's a slightly new twist on an old idea.

The idea for "Christmas Present" was actually my mother's; she suggested a story in which the ghost of the cat is identified by the scritching of claws in the doormat and the clink of the name tag on the food bowl. The vulgar bit is all mine however.

The beginning of "Overnight Bus" is an actual bus journey I took in South Africa. The bit where it goes strange in the middle is inspired by a short story called "Blessmans", about a bar in a foreign town, which I have read more than once in at least one anthology, and which I cannot now locate. Which given the nature of "Blessmans" is entirely appropriate.

"Indecent Behaviour" is the nastiest thing I've written. I don't like reading it; there is no gleam of light at all. Really, I suppose, it's about love, and how miserable it is to reject it utterly.

"Forward and Back, Change Places" is about folk-dancing and takes place at Cecil Sharp House, only slightly altered. I wrote it a long time ago and then wrote it again, hopefully much better. Don't tell people the ending.

"District to Upminster" was written for a train-related anthology. Of course the story is really one of those long Marty Feldman comedy sketches. With various bits of stock footage visible out of the window.

For "The Cupboard of Winds" I am entirely indebted to the late, great Paul Jennings (1918- 1989), writer, philosopher and humorist, the founder of Resistentialism ("Things are Against Us"), who wrote about the Loss Force and the Cupboard of the Winds. I have but taken a couple of his ideas and run with them, perhaps in an unexpected direction.

"Contamination" was written for a competition on Jo Fletcher's website, for a short story of not more than 140 words. It is two words short.

"Eyes of God": hundreds of years ago I read a piece in an old magazine about pre-Columbian pots that seemed to represent people disfigured to look like potatoes, and I wanted to write something about the worship of potatoes. When I saw a call for submissions to an anthology about potatoes, the time was clearly right.

"Dead Men's Company" was intended as an antidote to those movies where the pirate kidnaps the governor's daughter and after swearing at him for an hour and a half she falls for him in the last reel. Unlikely, thinks I – suppose it were the other way round... Thanks to Rychard Winslade for some nautical terms. The Brecht reference is trivial but it amused me. I think there's also a dash of Thomas Burke's story, "The Hollow Man", about a dead bloke that turns up in a cafe.

"Meeting at the Silver Dollar", obviously, is set in the fantasy world of Western movies, which made the imaginative landscape of my childhood. The story tips its hat to more films than you could shake a stick at.

Acknowledgements

All stories © Marion Pitman 2015

Publication History

"The Seal Songs" *19 magazine* © 1979: *Animal Ghosts* © 1980

"Amenities" *The City magazine* © 2000

"Sunlight in Spelling" *3SF magazine* © 2002

"Disposal of the Body" *Corpseblossoms* © 2005

"Saxophony" *Subtle Edens* © 2008

"Out of Season" *Shades of Darkness* © 2008

"The Washing of the Waters" *Wildstacks* © 2011

"Music in the Bone" *Eighth Black Book of Horror* © 2011

"Looking Glass" *Estronomicon* © 2011

"Christmas Present" *Estronomicon* © 2011

"Contamination" (runner up in competition on Jo Fletcher website) © 2011

"Overnight Bus" *Where are we Going?* © 2012

"Forward and Back, Change Places" *Hauntings* © 2012

"Indecent Behaviour" *Ninth Black Book of Horror* © 2012

"District to Upminster" *Rustblind and Silverbright* © 2013

"Meeting at the Silver Dollar" *Alchemy Press Book of Pulp Heroes* 2 © 2013

"Cave Arborem" *Unspoken Water 4* © 2013

"Cupboard of the Winds" *Alchemy Press Book of Urban Mythic 2* © 2014

"Eyes of God" *Potatoes* © 2014

"Dead Men's Company" previously unpublished © 2015

www.ingramcontent.com/pod-product-compliance
Lightning Source LLC
LaVergne TN
LVHW041704060526
838201LV00043B/567